BEASTS

BEASTS

Joyce Carol Oates

CHIVERS
THORNDIKE

This Large Print edition is published by BBC Audiobooks Ltd, Bath, England and by Thorndike Press, Waterville, Maine, USA.

Published in 2004 in the U.K. by arrangement with Orion.

Published in 2004 in the U.S. by arrangement with Carroll & Graf Publishers, a division of Avalon Publishing Group, Inc.

U.K. Hardcover ISBN 0–7540–9919–9 (Chivers Large Print)
U.K. Softcover ISBN 0–7540–9920–2 (Camden Large Print)
U.S. Softcover ISBN 0–7862–6267–2 (General)

The text of this Large Print edition is unabridged.
Other aspects of the book may vary from the original edition.

Set in 16 pt. New Times Roman.

Printed in Great Britain on acid-free paper.

British Library Cataloguing in Publication Data available

Library of Congress Control Number : 2003115244

I love you, rotten,
Delicious rottenness.

. . . wonderful are the hellish experiences,
Orphic, delicate
Dionysos of the Underworld.

D. H. Lawrence, 'Medlars and Sorb-Apples'
from *Birds, Beasts and Flowers*

1. *Paris, France*

In the Oceania wing of the Louvre I saw it: the totem.

It was approximately ten feet high, a primitive, angular wooden figure, seemingly female, with a long, narrow brute face, blank eyes, and a slash for a mouth. Its breasts were exaggerated like a beast's dugs, foot-long wooden slats descending from the shoulders; against these breasts the figure clenched what appeared to be a nursing infant. Except the infant was only a head, grotesquely large and round; the infant had no body. The totem was identified simply as an aboriginal 'Maternal Figure' from British Columbia, Canada, at least two hundred years old.

There. There it is.

It wasn't burned after all . . .

I was confused, I wasn't thinking coherently. In the chilly, austere room in which the aboriginal totem was displayed it exuded an air so raw, elemental, primitive it seemed only minimally human. I stared at it, and shuddered. I turned away, wanting to leave, but found myself staring at the totem again, having returned to stand before it. As if the nursing mother had called to me . . . *Gillian?*

1

Don't be afraid. We are beasts, this is our consolation. For here was nightmare. Here was obscenity. I imagined how, staring at such a thing, a man might feel sexual desire wither and shrink within him: the yearning, hungry male reduced here to an ugly head, pressed so tight against the mother, it must surely smother. A woman would feel all softness within her, the tenderness that makes us human, vanish.

We are beasts, we feel no guilt.

Never guilt.

'Madame? Excuse me, but are you—all right?'

The voice was reassuringly American. A prosperous middle-aged Midwestern-looking gentleman who, with his concerned wife, had been observing me.

Quickly I said, my bright American smile like neon flashing, 'Thank you, you're very kind. But I'm fine.' I'd been stricken with light-headedness and may have been swaying on my feet. But now I was fine. And I didn't want to be approached, and I didn't want to be touched. The couple continued to stare at me so I repeated, 'Thank you!' and turned decisively away.

I left the Louvre, shaken. Blindly I walked along the Seine embankment. That totem! So ugly, and yet so powerful. And the eyes.

I was thinking of the deaths of two people I'd loved, a long time ago. They'd died

2

horribly, and their deaths were believed to be accidental.

The Parisian sky was opaque, the Seine was the color of lead. Far away the romantic spires of Notre Dame were nearly obscured in mist, or smog. I was so distracted I hardly noticed the venders' intrusive stalls blocking the view of the fabled river.

I was forty-four years old. A quarter-century had passed.

This is not a confession. You will see, I have nothing to confess.

2. The Alarm

20 JANUARY 1976

In the night, sirens erupting.
In the night, the terrible beauty of fire.
A night in midwinter. In bitter sub-zero cold. In the Berkshire Mountains in southwestern Massachusetts. Flames leaping skyward out of the densely wooded cul-de-sac of a gravel road bordering the college.

A deafening alarm was ringing in our residence. I believed I could smell smoke, my heart hammered in panic.

Still I had time to think, *This can't be happening.*

For it was never real to me. Never would it seem other than a confused dream.

I stumbled outside with the others. We were dazed like cattle stampeding. It was 3:50 A.M. It was fifteen degrees below zero. The icy wind blew smoke into our faces. My head ached with cold, where was my hair? What had happened to my hair? I touched my head, my close-cropped hair, and remembered.

My hair, too, was burning. My braided hair, so beautiful.

We saw: the fire was elsewhere. Not Heath Cottage. The alarm in our residence had been pulled in error. We should have felt relief, the

5

fire was a half-mile away.

Where? One of the faculty houses on Brierly Lane?

Some of us were crying. Like frightened children we gripped one another's icy hands. Yet there was an air of festivity, too. A fire? Oh, where? Hastily we'd thrown on coats and jackets, kicked our bare feet into boots. Panic made us silly, somehow. It was so cold, tears ran down our cheeks and began to freeze within seconds.

Beautiful husky Dominique grabbed me and licked away my frost-tears with her soft, warm tongue.

Proctors were telling us to return to the residence, we were in no danger. The fire was off-campus. Volunteer firemen from Catamount were already at the burning house. A second firetruck, bearing professional firefighters, would arrive from Great Barrington within a few minutes.

Still, the fire would burn 'out of control' for a lethal period of more than an hour.

By the time the fire had been reported by a Brierly Lane neighbor, it was burning intensely. By the time firemen deluged the roof with water, much of the roof had burned through.

Most of the houses on Brierly Lane were old New England farmhouses and colonials, made of wood and stucco. With steep, shingled roofs. Set back from the graveled road in dense thickets of juniper pines and birches. Driveways were narrow, making the approach of firetrucks difficult.

I hated the proctors shouting at us as if we were willful children. We were not children, we need not obey. Some of us wanted to slip past the proctors and make our way across campus, to Brierly Lane. To see for ourselves what was happening.

Whose house was burning.

Particles of soot were blown against our faces. Sticking in our eyelashes like tarry tears.

Someone, it might have been Cassie, squeezed my hand so hard I winced in pain. Though it was a happy, giddy, adrenaline-charged pain.

Whose house is it, burning?

Is it . . .?

We were being herded back inside Heath Cottage. Suddenly I was very tired, I wanted to lie down on the stairs and sleep. I wanted only to be safe inside, in the lighted warmth. My knees were shaking. I stumbled on the steps that seemed so steep suddenly, a friend caught me beneath the arms. I was such a small girl, I weighed only ninety pounds. But don't be deceived.

Or maybe: I hadn't been awakened by the siren. I hadn't been awakened by the fire alarm. Or by the other girls' cries. In fact, I hadn't slept yet that night, I'd been lying partly undressed in my cot-sized bed, Catamount

7

College-issue with no frills, a metal frame, lumpy mattress, and no headboard, writing in my journal notebook as I'd been commanded. *Go for the jugular.*

3. My (Secret) Journal

'Dor-cas.'

I whispered the name to myself.

I was following the woman through a hilly wooded area, along a path strewn with pine needles into the village of Catamount, Massachusetts. My third year at Catamount College. The woman called herself, with arrogant simplicity, 'Dorcas.' She had no idea that anyone was following her. She had no idea of my existence. She was the wife of a man I believed I loved. *Loved more than life itself,* I might have said.

The conviction, or maybe it was the sensation, to which I gave the name *love*, coursed through my veins like liquid flame.

Dorcas! Andre Harrow's wife. Unsuspecting of being followed, so raptly observed. How astonished Dorcas would have been, how annoyed. Amused?

This wasn't the first time I'd followed Dorcas. It was maybe the fifth or sixth time, for my infatuation with Andre Harrow had begun the previous spring, during my sophomore year at the college. Yet I seemed to know that there would be something different about today, this afternoon. That possibly I would make a mistake, and regret it. Or maybe: it wouldn't be a mistake.

Recall the excitement. Almost unbearable tension/pleasure. Following another person in secret. I want to note this here in my journal. Even if it's only for myself.

I saw that Dorcas was carrying parcels. I supposed she was headed for the 'historic' post office in Catamount. She'd decided to walk from her house on Brierly Lane instead of driving, it was such a brightly chilly, beautiful New England autumn day.

Smelling of juniper pines. Pine needles underfoot.

I had not intended this. I had not wished to follow Andre Harrow's wife. Yet, as soon as I stepped out of the chapel and saw her, across the grassy quadrangle, I knew I had no choice. *There! There she is.* Each time it happened like this. Five or six times and each time the first. I saw the russet-red hair and the unmistakably indolent, luxuriant motions of a mature woman's body among the slender, faster-moving Catamount students. Dorcas, majestic, aloof, moving at her slow pace, oblivious of them.

Yet few were oblivious of her. You couldn't not notice Dorcas. Especially those girls who recognized her, and knew to whom she was married.

Look! Dorcas.

The sculptress? That's her?

10

Andre Harrow's wife?

If you love a married man you exist in a special, secret, undeclared relationship with his wife.

I was twenty years old when it began. I believed that no one knew, no one guessed. I did not want to approach the man; I dared not. In the chapel, which was a place of stark, chaste, white walls, a minimal altar draped in white like a tablecloth, and no religious iconography to hint that Catamount College had once been, before the revolutionary sixties, a Presbyterian-founded women's college, I told myself sternly that it was a hopeless infatuation I felt for Andre Harrow; worse than hopeless, it was demeaning. What would my mother think? My distant, aging father? I told myself, *No more!* In the chapel I never prayed (for I didn't believe in God—did I?) but I assumed the posture, and the attitude, of prayer. I hid my face in my hands, I shut my eyes tight. *I want to be good. I want to be sensible, sane.* I resolved not to brood upon Andre Harrow anymore, and not to be distracted by thoughts of his wife.

(You would wonder that I could be so emotionally inexperienced, or undernourished, as well as sexually immature, at the age of twenty, in 1975. I'd been born in 1955 and had come into consciousness during the 1960s, the most sexually 'liberated,' 'amoral' era in United States history.)

11

Then: I left the chapel, stepped outside squinting in the sunshine, and immediately sighted the woman—Dorcas!—across the quadrangle. At once, my resolutions fell away. I forgot them entirely. I hurried to follow Dorcas as if she'd called to me. What choice had I?

I was drawn in the woman's wake like a fluttering scrap of paper in the wake of a rushing vehicle.

Quickly I crossed a corner of the quadrangle, keeping Dorcas in sight. If she happened to glance around, which, being Dorcas, she wouldn't have done, I could be assured that she wouldn't take notice of me.

These small adventures were not premeditated, as you can see. They were not willed. I was no predator seeking prey, I was myself the prey. I was the innocent party.

On the sidewalk, about thirty feet behind Dorcas, I took care to hide for as long as I could behind knots of other girls headed in the same general direction. The chapel bell was tolling three. I had intended to go to the library but I followed Dorcas past the glassy-glittering facade of the library, and past the administration building. I heard someone call out, 'Gillian? Going this way?'—a girl named Sybil, from my Renaissance lecture class. Quickly I smiled and shook my head no, no I was not. Not going your way. Not right now.

Goddamn, I'd almost lost Dorcas! Girls

milling on the walk outside the Life Sciences Building, smoking. Blocking my view.

The campus was small: less than three thousand students. Yet at times it seemed crowded, you saw the same faces often. You walked in the same pattern. I didn't want anyone who knew me to see me. I was fearful that, if one of my friends sighted Dorcas, and then me, she would know exactly what I was doing.

I'd crossed down behind the Life Sciences Building. Trotted through a parking lot. It was hilly here, descending to Catamount Creek. I picked up Dorcas on a downward path, like a hunting dog picking up a scent. I'd surmised by this time where she was headed, into the village. I wouldn't lose her again.

You should be ashamed. This is shame!

Yes, it was shame. And yet: so much more.

*   *   *

Dorcas was an artist, a sculptress. You admired her work or hated it. You admired her or hated her. It was that simple, and yet it wasn't simple at all.

WE ARE BEASTS AND THIS IS OUR CONSOLATION

These provocative words Dorcas had affixed boldly to a wall of the college art museum, to accompany her sculpture exhibit *Totem & Taboo* in the spring of 1975.

Dorcas was 'Dorcas'—no surname. It wasn't a secret that she was Andre Harrow's wife, of course, but no one would have dreamt of calling her 'Mrs. Harrow.'

Such an appellation as 'Mrs.' was ludicrous in reference to Dorcas. You couldn't imagine her belonging to any man.

There was some mystery or secret—or there was a rumor of a mystery or secret—regarding Dorcas's children, or child. It seemed to be known, but vaguely, that Dorcas was a 'mother'—that Dorcas had had children, or a child. Not with Andre Harrow? In a time predating her arrival in Catamount?

She and Andre Harrow had come to Catamount College in the mid-1960s. Mr. Harrow had the rank of Professor, Dorcas was not on the faculty and was said to scorn academic life.

As she scorned conventional bourgeois life.

Her sculptures! They were made of wood, larger than life-sized, primitive and dramatic. They were raw, crude, ugly. Most were of women, and were defiantly sexual, with protuberant breasts and bellies, exaggerated pudenda. Rounded buttocks, with a crevicelike crack between. Heads tended to be small, and faces minimal. Like others I was disturbed by these figures, and excited. I remember when I saw them for the first time, I was literally openmouthed. It wouldn't occur to me until years later that Dorcas's primitive totems, and the aesthetic concept behind the art, were not original in 1975. (But then, in the chaos of contemporary art, what is original?) It was said of Dorcas that she sawed, sanded, chiseled, and carved the totems out of hunks of untreated wood, that she worked by hand, her hands lacerated by splinters, her fingernails broken. It was said that Dorcas had few friends in Catamount, even among the artists, but that from time to time she accepted an 'intern' to help in her studio, sometimes even to model. She and Andre Harrow sometimes befriended Catamount girls—'special' girls.

I was jealous, I don't deny it. I believed I knew two or three of these girls. I wasn't certain. There was an air of secrecy about this. It was said that if a girl behaved as if she were on intimate terms with Mr. Harrow, or dropped Dorcas's name casually, it meant just the opposite.

Another statement Dorcas had affixed to a museum wall was:

TRUST NOT IN APPEARANCES NOR IN
WHAT LIES BENEATH

And so, you either admired Dorcas or hated her. Angry Catamount alums protested *Totem & Taboo* as if the sculptures were personally threatening. There was a letter-writing campaign —furious letters appeared for weeks in the college paper—denouncing the 'so-called "artist" Dorcas' and her work that was 'disgusting,' 'depraved,' 'a travesty of beauty,' 'a travesty of decency,' 'a stain on the reputation of Catamount College.' One of the alums, Class of '49, demanded to know, 'Who is a BEAST? . . . Who dares to call us BEASTS?' Another, Class of '39, proclaimed, 'We are not beasts who have been proudly created in God's likeness and possess immortal souls.' A number of wealthy alums threatened to withhold donations unless the offensive art was immediately removed. (To their credit, the college administrators refused to give in.) You'd have thought, considering that Catamount College was nearly as liberal by 1975 as Bennington College, that the overwhelming majority of Catamount students would have defended Dorcas, but there were a number of demonstrative students who hated *Totem & Taboo* as much as the alums. They called it 'gross,' 'putrid,' 'sexist,' 'a betrayal of feminism.' During the exhibit of four harried weeks the museum wing was continuously littered with crumpled and torn *Totem & Taboo* brochures. There was graffiti on some of the totem pedestals and someone had gone so far as to deface a squatting birth figure by scrawling 'BULLSHIT' in red nail polish across the figure's massive belly. The defacing was something of a local scandal, and attracted

16

the attention of the *New York Times,* but Dorcas stubbornly insisted upon keeping the birth figure as it was. In her interview in the *Times* Dorcas inflamed more observers by saying, 'Vandalism to a work of art is its own art. I love insult, it's always honest.'

What a thing to say! I laughed aloud, when I heard this.

Of course, Dorcas was correct.

*   *   *

I returned to the exhibit several times. I never knew whether I admired Dorcas's wooden figures, or detested them. I never knew whether they excited me as works of art—for I thought of myself as an artist too, a poet—or whether they repulsed me. For they were so ugly, so un-, or anti-, *feminine.*

Was that a good thing, or not so good a thing?

On my final visit, in May, seeing that I was alone in the gallery, I felt a sudden impulse to deface one of the figures myself. The one I hated most was an angular adolescent girl of my approximate height, five feet, with a blank, rather simian face, a smallish bald head, tiny Dixie-cup breasts, and an angular, bony pelvis. The figure's sexual organs were visible, though very small. *Look at me, why are you ashamed to look at me?* the figure seemed to be taunting. A flame passed over my brain. I hated the ugly

17

thing! I removed a fluorescent-orange marker pen from my backpack, approached the figure tremulously, and stood before it for several minutes trying to summon up the courage to deface it. How I hated it and how I hated Dorcas who was the wife of Andre Harrow who was the man I loved and who would never love me, would never so much as glance at me, for I was not female in the way that Dorcas was female, my body was like that of the totem titled, 'Girl' and not like that of Dorcas herself. Yet, if I defaced the totem, how would Dorcas respond? *I love insult, it's always honest.* The adolescent figure seemed to be telling me that, too. Taunting me. The flat, monkeyish face that bore just a faint, caricatured resemblance to my own face, the eyes that were uneven sightless holes bored into wood, the grim yet self-satisfied slash of a mouth. *Your mirror-twin. Why hate me?* How could this be? I was frightened; the sense of kinship, of an almost physical rapport, came so strong.

I returned the Magic Marker to my backpack.

Now, I was annoyed that recent visitors to the exhibit had left the usual litter. Why hadn't anyone cleaned up? There were crumpled brochures on the totems themselves as well as on the floor. One by one I collected them and tossed them into a wastebasket. My face burned, I was incensed on behalf of Dorcas.

18

Absorbed in my task I began to feel someone watching me. *It's her. Dorcas?* But when I turned, no one was there.

*   *   *

Dorcas wasn't a fast walker. It was difficult for me to keep behind her. I tried to let others, joggers and bicyclists, come between us. I followed her past a field where girls were playing soccer, and into the woods bordering Catamount Creek. The smell of pine needles underfoot was sharp, pungent. I seemed to know that I would always associate that smell with this afternoon, and with Dorcas.

It was a ten-minute walk from campus into the village. I'd begun to perspire even though in the woods, out of the direct sun, the air was chilly. I told myself I could turn back at any moment. I told myself, *This is more than shame, this is folly.* In the village, on Mill Street leading up to Main, I saw several men, local residents unconnected with the college, glance at Dorcas, turn in passing, and frankly stare. I wondered if they knew her, or if they were responding simply to her appearance. Clearly she aroused their interest, their disapproval, their resentment, possibly their admiration. They would figure her as a hippie—an 'artist-type.' For Dorcas didn't offer herself passively to be judged, like most women. She wasn't one to shrink from the rude stares of men; scarcely

19

would she acknowledge their presence. She was a woman in her late thirties of ample proportions who exulted in her body, believing herself beautiful and desirable even if, in ignorant eyes, she might be repellent.

At the corner of Mill and Main, I saw a man approach Dorcas. He was middle-aged but youngish, in stained workclothes and boots. His face was flushed, he had a two- or three-day beard. He was saying something that Dorcas, quickening her stride, chose to ignore. When I drew nearer I heard him cursing after her. I heard him saying what sounded like, 'Think I don't know who you are? Think I don't know you? Fuck *you*.'

I had no choice but to closely pass by this angry man on the sidewalk. His eyes flicked onto me unseeing. The flush in his cheeks deepened. How did he know Dorcas, I wondered; what could be their connection? It would have seemed to anyone who knew Dorcas and Andre Harrow that they'd have had little connection with Catamount residents.

Dorcas, ahead, glanced back to see if the man was following her. He wasn't. She took no more notice of me than if I'd been invisible.

I was now following Dorcas more openly on Main Street. For I, too, was on my way to the post office; this was a likely destination for a Catamount student. I reasoned that I had as much purpose here as anyone. By the time

20

Dorcas and I reached the steps of the post office, my heart was beating painfully. I hesitated before hurrying up the steps to hold the heavy door as Dorcas, parcels in her arms, stepped inside. She murmured what sounded like an airy 'Thank you'—her expression showing the annoyance we feel for a stranger, however well-intentioned, who has intruded upon our privacy.

I was surprised that Dorcas was out of breath, nearly panting. The post-office steps were steep and she was overweight by perhaps thirty pounds. Her short upper lip was dewy with perspiration. I smelled her rich scent— the warm, yeasty, female body. Usually Dorcas wore her hair loose on her shoulders, wavy and rippling, but that day she'd coiled it into a careless French twist that was loosening now in wisps and strands. Close up, I saw that Dorcas was wearing handwrought aluminum earrings that swung like scimitars from her pinkened ears. Chunky silver rings gleamed on her fingers. Her nails were short as a man's, ridged with dirt or black paint. She'd made up her face in her usual lavish style, with an artist's skill and what may have been an artist's wit, for perhaps Dorcas, living in a small New England college town in 1975, was meant to suggest a sloe-eyed, savage-voluptuous female portrait by Picasso of the early years of the twentieth century. Dorcas's eyebrows were thick, dark, and chiseled; her lips, painted purplish-crimson with a distinct outline in a deeper shade, were swollen-looking; her shrewd eyes, almond-shaped, were outlined in sticky black mascara. Her face was a mask of pale, grainy powder like a geisha's. She wore her usual denim smock with paint-stained cuffs, a long denim skirt stencilled in rainbow colors, and leather sandals that displayed her startlingly small, attractive bare feet. (With blue-polished toenails.) Around her fleshy shoulders, to complete this costume, she'd tied a coarse-knit, parrot-green shawl with fringes halfway down her back. Dorcas was sexy, seductive. She was big-breasted, big-hipped. When she walked, her buttocks swayed. It was impossible not to stare at her, as customers in the post office were doing.

At the counter Dorcas spoke to the clerk in a raised, bossy voice; her English was French-accented. Her transactions took some time; the line behind her grew. When finally she turned, she saw me standing a few yards away, with no excuse now except that I was watching her. Dorcas hadn't taken any real notice of me before, and now she approached me as she might have approached a curious-looking child. Her almond eyes lost their sardonic luster and widened with interest. Was it my hair? My long, wavy hair was my most striking feature. It fell several inches past my shoulders in a scintillant tangle. It was hair to hide behind, to wrap myself in. It was a mix of dark brown, wheat-color, strawberry blond, russet-red, and even silver. Everyone in my mother's family went prematurely gray: this was my fate. Boldly Dorcas touched my hair, smoothing and stroking it. I stood paralyzed, not daring to breathe. To herself she murmured, *'Belle. Très belle.'* She surprised me by gripping thick strands of my hair in both hands and lifting them beside my head, straight out, and staring at me appraisingly. In her playful, French-accented English she said, 'And which one of them are *you*?'

4. *The Fires*

At Catamount College in the foothills of the Berkshire Mountains, in southwest Massachusetts in the gauzy aftermath of the Vietnam War that was the mid-1970s, there had been several small, mysterious fires. Local authorities had determined each of the fires to be arson, but no arsonist or arsonists had yet been identified. So far, in the fall of my junior year, the fires had been confined to areas of the campus, like the main dining hall after closing, where no one was likely to be injured. Oily rags were set aflame in a trash can behind the eighteenth-century colonial that housed the Humanities Department, in fact, just below the second-floor office of Professor Andre Harrow, but this, too, had been during the night. There was a similar fire of oily rags set in a vestibule of the administration building, and smoldering books in a remote corner of the college library (subject: pre-Socratic Greek philosophy) set off fire alarms and sprinklers that sent everyone in the building, including me, rushing panicked for the exits; but, except for a girl who fell and broke her ankle, no one was injured.

Yet we never knew, when we went to bed at

night, whether we'd be wakened by alarms, and whether the alarms would be false or real. We never knew whether our own residence might be burning. We never knew (we told each other, with grim humor) whether we might be 'burned alive' in our beds.

No one seemed to know, or would acknowledge, who was doing these things, or why. Political activism at Catamount, as at other colleges and universities, had virtually ceased since the end of the Vietnam War. The Age of Ignominy was over. There was little for us to protest now, and little energy with which to protest. My college generation was conceded to be 'apathetic' if not 'anesthetized.' At Catamount College, the youngish president had helped in Eugene McCarthy's campaign; she and her senior administrators had come of age in the 1960s and were considered liberal, if not, in some quarters, radical. And so: why set fires at Catamount, of all colleges? What was the symbolism, what was the purpose?

Clearly, it had to be a private purpose.

Catamount Township fire investigators had come to the conclusion that a single individual had probably set the fires, while others, probably unrelated to the arsonist, were setting alarms as pranks. You heard rumors . . . I had no idea who the arsonist was but her random acts seemed to me logical, like a message in code. In my journal I wrote,

26

She's in love, too. They scorn her. They look through her, invisible.

*   *   *

'Who d'you think is doing these things?'
   'She's sick, whoever. She needs help.'
   'She needs to be thrown in jail!'
   'Could be a "he."'
   'No. It's one of us. I have a feeling.'
One of us. One of us Catamount students.
I, too, thought so. I, too, had a 'feeling.'

So, wakened by alarms and commotion on campus, we discussed the mysterious fires. Dominique, and Penelope, and Marisa, and Cassandra ('Cassie,' whose room was next to mine on the third floor of the residence), and Gillian (me). Our residence, Heath Cottage, was the smallest dormitory on campus; it was no cottage in fact but one of the college's old, charmingly rundown colonial houses, with sloping floors, tall, narrow, ill-fitting windows, faded pancake-thin Oriental rugs said to be priceless antiques, and poor insulation to protect us against the New England winter. 'Our tinderbox,' we called it. Even the outdoor fire escapes were aged, rusted.

So far, however, Heath Cottage had been spared. There were only twelve of us living there, and all of us connected in some way with the arts: creative writing, theater, dance, music. No false alarms had been set in Heath

27

Cottage—yet. But we were edgy and anxious like everyone else.

Waiting for something to happen.

'My theory is, she doesn't want anybody to be actually *hurt*.'

'Which means, what? It's all a joke?'

'No. She wants attention.'

'Like trying to kill yourself? They say most times it's "a cry for help."'

'I'll give that bitch a "cry for help," if I find out who it is. I can't sleep anymore, I'm so *nervous*.'

'Me too. I'm lying there in the dark, trying to keep my eyes shut, imagining I smell smoke.'

'Well, whoever it is, she's got to be sick. It is a kind of suicide.'

'If a guy was doing it, what'd it be? Not suicide, I bet.'

'For a guy it's something, like, sexy, right? Guys get off on fires.'

'But not girls? Not women?'

Dominique laughed sharply. 'For sure, not *me*.'

But we wondered: was it so? Wasn't it so? Why not? *Why?*

'Something to do with sex, I guess. For a guy.'

'For women, sex is personal. You think of a *person*.'

'Are all women the same? Like, think of those wooden sculptures of Dorcas's.'

'Ugh! Those ugly things! They should

28

be burned.'

'No. They're strong, they're meant to empower women. The idea is, we're all animals and that's our strength.'

It was Marisa who spoke with such vehemence. We glanced at her, uneasily.

Cassie said, 'I still think it could be a male. Like from outside? Somebody who resents us, hates us. You know, "college girls." Some asshole who thinks we're all rich, spoiled, that kind of crap.'

'How'd a guy from town get into the library and not be seen? It has to be someone who's a student here. Who fits right in. Just one of *us*.'

'Except, hey: not *us*. Not literally *us*.'

We looked anxiously at one another. We laughed. We were certain, we were absolutely certain, that the arsonist might be a student at Catamount College but she wasn't one of us, residents of Heath Cottage.

'My idea is: she's in love. She's sick, she's crazy in love.'

'In love with . . . who?'

There was a silence. Marisa giggled nervously. Dominique blew her nose. I felt my face burn and knew that a humiliating blush was lifting into my cheeks like an outspread hand.

Each of us was thinking *Andre Harrow. But we must not utter the name.*

5. 'Peach'

Sometimes you fall in love without knowing. Without realizing. And it's too late, and you can't undo it.

Last March my mother called me to inform me—that was her word, 'inform'—that my father had 'taken a separate residence' and that he would be 'contacting' me soon. I'd had a vague uneasy awareness that my parents' marriage was worm-riddled like old rotted wood but still this came as a surprise. You could say it came as a shock. I may have cried. A little. My mother said sharply, 'Tears won't help, Gillian. They've never helped me.'

I hung up the phone with Mother still talking. If she called back, I wasn't in my room to hear the phone ring.

This was before voice mail, recorded phone messages you can't escape. Life was easier then. You just didn't pick up the phone.

But that night when I finally got to sleep I didn't dream about my father. I dreamt of a man whose face I couldn't see clearly but I was allowed to know *He loves me. He will care for me.* The dream was crowded and confused like most of my dreams, a jumbled landscape through which I was running, or trying to run; the air was thick and suffocating and I was trying so very hard to run, my heart pounded

30

with the effort. But there was a man, with a blurred, luminous face. I understood that he was a kindly man, he spoke to me in a low, confiding, consoling voice, a voice I felt rather than heard, a voice that made me suddenly so happy for I knew *You will be all right, Gillian, you will be loved, I will care for you.*

But I knew I must not tell anyone. For this man, who was one of my professors, could not love his other students as he loved me, and so it was unfair, it was wrong, I must never tell of his love for me or his love would vanish. I was crying now, *I will never tell anyone, Mr. Harrow.* And he lifted me in his arms, as my father had not lifted me in fifteen years; he kissed me gently on the lips, and a great happiness suffused me like a blessing.

*   *   *

Mr. Harrow was reading to us. In his low, gravelly voice like a rough caress. Where our other professors were likely to be brisk and ironic and show-offy, Mr. Harrow was sincere, and made us squirm sometimes with his candor. One of his heroes was D. H. Lawrence. He read to us the blithe, lovely poem 'Peach' from Lawrence's *Birds, Beasts and Flowers,* and the poem's sensuous language was like an incantation.

31

Why so velvety, why so voluptuous heavy?
Why hanging with such inordinate weight?
Why so dented?
Why the groove?
Why the lovely, bivalve roundnesses?
Why the ripple down the sphere?
Why the suggestion of incision?

In rapt astonishment I listened. I was seated in the front row in Mr. Harrow's large lecture class of about one hundred fifty students and I was staring intently at Mr. Harrow and I realized that, though I'd read 'Peach' previously, as I'd read numerous other poems by D. H. Lawrence, I had not understood it until now. Until hearing it in Mr. Harrow's voice. In Mr. Harrow's voice which was itself velvety, voluptuous-heavy. It seemed to me that as he read, Mr. Harrow glanced up to look at me. It seemed to me that Mr. Harrow was himself the poet and the words of the poem were his words, intimate and shocking. And consoling. For I understood now that the true subject of the poem wasn't a peach, a peach devoured by the poet, a peach he finds delicious, juice running down his fingers, the true subject of the poem was the female body.
The female genitals. The vagina.
That secret femaleness at the core of a woman's being, hidden from the world. Hidden, because it is fearful of being injured.
Hidden because it is fearful of being

32

mocked. Derided as ugly.

Some of the girls in the class were laughing nervously. They understood, too. The poet was making us feel this delicious intimacy, this sensuous unspoken truth, that the female body harbors unexpected beauty, that we must not be ashamed of our bodies but proud of them. We should exult in them. I felt my eyes sting with tears. Not the tears provoked by Mother's telephone call of the previous day, but tears of happiness in my dream. For the voice of my professor Andre Harrow was the very voice of my dream, unmistakable.

Gillian, you will be loved. I will care for you.

Was I imagining this? I was not.

The remainder of the class hour passed by in a blur. A buzzing radiance. I saw how often Professor Harrow glanced at me, how he seemed to be smiling at me with his eyes. He told the raptly listening class frankly, not as if he were lecturing but as if he were simply talking to us, confiding in us, stroking his short spade-shaped beard that resembled D. H. Lawrence's, 'Lawrence is the supreme poet of Eros. No recriminations, no reproaches, no guilt, no "morality." For what's "morality" but a leash around the neck? A noose? What's "morality" but what other people want you to do, for their own selfish, unstated purposes?' Mr. Harrow paused. Again it seemed that he was looking at me, smiling with his eyes. He was a lean, lanky man with a quicksilver manner, energetic, restless. He was no age I might have guessed—thirty-five? thirty-seven?—at least twenty years younger than my remote, fading father. *My father I hated, I wished might die. Of a heart attack, quickly, to spare Mother and me shame.* Mr. Harrow was saying, concluding, 'Lawrence teaches us that love-sensual, sexual, physical love—is the reason we exist. He detested "dutiful" love—for parents, family, country, God. He was in fact a deeply religious man but he celebrated, not a dead God, but a living Eros. He tells us "Love should be intense, individual,/Not boundless./This boundless love is like a bad smell."'

* * *

That afternoon when I returned to my dormitory there was a pink slip in my mailbox. I should call my mother at once. With trembling fingers I tore the slip into pieces. 'What do I care for *her*, or for *him*?' It did seem to me that familial love was mere duty: a bad smell. I would make plans to spend most of the summer in Maine, as a counsellor in a camp for mildly disabled children; I would avoid visiting either of my parents. I was in love now. I took strength from my love for Mr. Harrow. Though knowing, for I was no fool, that it could never be reciprocated.

This was March 1975.

34

6.

OCTOBER 1975

Philomela he called me.
Philomela, the girl without a tongue.
It was a joke, I think. But not a cruel joke.

*   *   *

Because I was ridiculously shy in his presence.
Because, unlike the others, I could not bring
myself to call him 'Andre.'

*   *   *

At Catamount College there were only two
faculty ranks: Instructor and Professor. Andre
Harrow, whose rank was Professor, who'd been
arrested in anti-Vietnam War demonstrations
in Washington, D.C., and who publicly
repudiated rank, privilege, artificial distinctions
like academic titles ('the residue of bourgeois
self-aggrandizement'), insisted that Catamount
students call him, not Professor, but Mister.

He urged students in his elite, small classes
to call him 'Andre.'

Andre! I could no more have called Mr.
Harrow by his first name than I could have
called my parents by their first names. This

35

would have been to me a violation of a principle of authority. The equivalent of raking my fingernails down a blackboard.

(It had long been impossible for me to call my parents even 'Mom,' 'Dad.' In our austere household these figures of authority were perennially 'Mother,' 'Father.' You would wonder how, as an infant, I'd managed such ludicrous formalities, but truly I couldn't recall ever having called my parents anything else.)

In our poetry writing workshop of only ten students, selected out of a reputed forty applicants, several of the more brazen girls like Dominique, Marisa, and Sybil called Mr. Harrow 'Andre' as if such familiar usage were utterly natural. It amused me—well, it made me hot with jealousy, too—to see how my friends shamelessly leaned toward Mr. Harrow, drawing up their shoulders pertly to display their breasts, turning their faces at subtle, sly angles. *Look at me! Love me.* Dominique laughed her husky throaty naughty-girl laugh to capture Mr. Harrow's attention; Marisa repeatedly brushed her long ash-blond hair out of her eyes. Sybil pouted when workshop criticism was harsh on her poetry, like a child on the brink of furious tears whom Daddy must placate. There was even plain-faced humorless Catherine, cornering Mr. Harrow after class with her contrived questions. 'Mr. Harrow—I mean, A-Andre—what does this last line in "Leda and the Swan m-mean?' My heart contracted in disdain, I could not compete with these girls, and would not.

In love at a distance, so much of life has to be invented.

In love at a distance, you learn the strategies of indirection.

For even close-up, a few feet from Andre Harrow, I was distanced from him. I, Gillian Brauer, who managed to speak coherently and intelligently in my other classes, was made speechless by this man. I could not stare openly at him as I'd done in last spring's lecture course but I was keenly aware of him, every nuance of his expression, every remark, during the ninety minutes of our workshop; sometimes I scarcely heard what was being said by the others, or what criticism, astute or ignorant, was being directed at my poetry. (I'd been writing poetry since the age of fifteen. To me, poetry was a formal challenge: not to express 'myself,' but to create a poem crafted of intriguing, unusual words.) Sometimes my eyes filled unexpectedly with tears. *I am so happy my heart might burst.*

And why? Andre Harrow wasn't 'handsome': his skin was somewhat coarse, his face narrow and angular. His eyes were his most striking feature, a steely, luminous gray-green, looking as if they might glow in the dark; but there was a minuscule blood speck beside the iris of his right eye. He was lean, lanky, restless. There was something ferretlike about him, an animal impatient with confinement. The spade-shaped beard was sometimes unkempt, his longish, graying-brown hair was often greasy and fell about his face in quills. His teeth were uneven and, like his restless fingers, nicotine-stained. In our small seminar room he smoked Dutch-manufactured cigarillos that gave off an acrid odor, like smoldering corncobs; unconsciously, he let ashes drop onto the table and floor. (Most of the class smoked. This was 1975. Even Catherine, who had respiratory problems, and Sybil, whose father had died of lung cancer from smoking. Dominique and Marisa were both dancers, yet practically chain-smokers. Shall I confess, I'd have liked to smoke, too? The practice seemed to me sophisticated, seductive. I envied the aplomb with which Dominique and Marisa tumbled their packs of cigarettes and lighters out of their handbags and onto the table. I envied the way in which the smokers casually offered cigarettes to one another, or begged them; my heart was pierced with jealousy at the sight of Marisa, silky hair falling about her face, as she leaned into the erotic ritual of touching her cigarette, gripped between her lipsticked lips, to Mr. Harrow's flaming match, actually daring to cup her small hands about his big-knuckled hands, and luxuriously inhaling. 'Andre, thanks!' I envied the smokers but couldn't emulate them; smoking stung my eyes, and made me cough. I was a child playing with grown-ups' toys.)

Andre Harrow was verbose, bullying. He was kind, and condescending. He was forever interrupting us even as he urged us to 'speak your own mind—or someone else will speak it for you.' When he talked he became enlivened, and perspired; he wiped his flushed face, and beneath his nose, with the blunt edge of his hand; he gave off an odor of frank masculine sweat, like an overheated horse. Unlike our other professors who remained seated during class or stood rigidly behind podiums, Mr. Harrow was always leaping to his feet when an idea struck him. He paced about, gesturing, talking animatedly, a glisten in his face. His eyes raked ours.

At Catamount it was believed that Andre Harrow knew 'everything.' That is, Andre Harrow knew everything that was worthy of being known. The aphorisms of Nietzsche, delivered in a staccato voice: 'What is done for love always takes place beyond good and evil'; 'There are no moral phenomena, only a moral interpretation of phenomena.' He recited passages of poetry from Blake, Shelley, Whitman, Yeats, and Lawrence, with such fervor you understood that poetry was worth dying for. (Yet Mr. Harrow wasn't a poet himself, it seemed. We wondered why.)

Mr. Harrow dressed casually, yet with a certain swagger. He wore jeans with cashmere blazers, khakis with beautifully handknit sweaters. He wore black T-shirts that fitted his narrow, tightly muscled torso snugly; he wore a leather belt with a prominent silver buckle that drew attention to his almost unnaturally slender waist. He wore jogging shoes, hiker's boots. In warm weather, sandals. On only moderately sunny days he wore tropical-dark sunglasses as if light hurt his eyes.

Sometimes his humor could be cruel (he quoted lines from our poetry to expose their weakness) but he was never malicious. If we wiped at our eyes, if we bit our lips to keep from crying, we were flattered, too.

He cares. He thinks of me. I have meaning to him.

* * *

That afternoon he turned suddenly to me.

'And you, Philomela: what have you to say? You've been cryptically silent for the past hour.'

Philomela! Everyone in the seminar laughed.

We'd been reading selections from Ovid's *Metamorphoses*. Philomela was one of Ovid's brutally despoiled virgins who'd—literally—lost her tongue, and was eventually metamorphosed into a bird. It was witty of Mr. Harrow to call me by this name, if a bit bullying. Philomela had suffered a terrible fate

40

and there really was nothing funny about the fact that she'd become mute.

Still, I laughed. I laughed with the others. I managed to say something reasonably intelligent in response to Mr. Harrow's query but my face burned as if I'd been slapped. *As if I'd been slapped by Andre Harrow.*

'See? Philomela can be articulate when she wishes. When she's forced.' Mr. Harrow spoke almost coldly, stroking his stubby beard.

This time, laughter in the seminar room was slightly uneasy.

Of course, it was a joke. A teasing rebuke to Gillian who sat so silently while others plunged in and talked. In a small workshop, any student who sits mute is an annoyance to her teacher, and something of a threat: he wonders what she's thinking, and why she won't share her thoughts with the others. Mr. Harrow could have had no idea (could he?) how I adored him; how I fantasized about him, in private; how, in his presence, I rarely spoke because no words of mine seemed adequate, worthy. If Mr. Harrow sensed my confusion at his nearness, he was gentlemanly enough to give no sign.

On a recent sheaf of my poems he'd scrawled, *You must be more vocal in class!*

Now, he was teasing me with 'Philomela.' It was a strange, tense moment. For in Mr. Harrow's rough, gravelly caressing voice, 'Philomela' was melodic and mysterious, a

41

term of endearment.

I was embarrassed, and confused. No one else in the workshop had been so singled out.

'Philomela. Come see me after class, eh?'

Mr. Harrow's office was on the second floor of the wood-frame Humanities Building, a high-ceilinged room with peeling walls and tall, narrow, old-fashioned windows. Taking a chair he offered me, beside his desk, I recalled how not long ago the unknown arsonist had set a fire in oily rags beneath Mr. Harrow's window. Had it been mere chance, or deliberate? *To get the man's attention. To warn him there was danger.*

Mr. Harrow spoke matter-of-factly. 'I hope I didn't embarrass you just now, Gillian. Philomela was a tragic figure, I suppose.'

I said, 'She didn't die, at least. She survived.'

'As a bird with "blood-colored" breast feathers.'

Mr. Harrow laughed, saying this. Why was it funny?

I found myself laughing, too. My heart was pounding so hard, I could scarcely breathe.

Everyone else in the workshop had spoken with Mr. Harrow in his office, more than once. Sometimes, girls were lined up outside in the corridor, some of them seated on the floor; Mr. Harrow had numerous students in his other class in twentieth-century modernism. Yet I'd never dared to enter this room. The closeness of the man seemed

42

almost frightening to me. I was in terror that he might see at a glance how I adored him. I was frowning, sitting stiffly; staring at the cluttered surface of Mr. Harrow's desk as he spoke of Ovid and of 'myths of metamorphosis.' His desk was covered in papers and books; there was a copy of *Rolling Stone* with a smirking photo of Mick Jagger on the cover; there was a manual Underwood typewriter, and an old crook-necked lamp. The walls were lined with bookshelves and the bookshelves were crammed. On the nearest windowsill was a two-foot, carved wooden figure, obviously one of Dorcas's: it was an adolescent girl closely resembling the one I'd so hated in the exhibit the previous spring, with a sloping forehead, small blank eyes, tiny breasts and narrow hips, a slight potbelly, thin arms and legs, long feet. The girl's pudenda was smooth and hairless, like her head; her genitals were suggested by delicate grooves in the wood. This time, I found the girl less repulsive. If you looked closely you could see something sly and sensual in her face. *Don't judge me without knowing me. My sister!*

'My wife says you were following her not long ago. In the village.'

This remark so took me by surprise, I couldn't speak. I stared at Mr. Harrow, stricken. The tiny blood speck floated in his eye.

'Of course, Dorcas exaggerates. She's a

dramatic woman. If she enmeshes you in her fantasies you become exaggerated, too.'

What did this mean? I smiled uneasily. I stammered, 'I wasn't following your wife, Mr. Harrow. I was on my way to the post office . . .' The lie made my face flame. But Andre Harrow seemed to be willing it. Of all things, he dreaded a halting, blushing confession of infatuation from one of his schoolgirl poets.

Of all things he dreaded an outburst of tears.

In a kindly voice he said, as if placating a child, 'Of course. It's common knowledge, Dorcas exaggerates.'

Mr. Harrow turned our conversation onto the workshop. The poetry we'd been reading, including Ovid, and my poetry. He lit up another of his Dutch cigarillos, and exhaled smoke in two thin streams. The corners of his eyes were lined as if he'd been squinting into the sun and his right incisor appeared to be chipped. After our intense two-hour workshop he seemed hardly tired, but restless.

'Gillian. Do you have any questions? I think you do.'

I stared at him uncomprehending.

Except: I did want to know why in Ovid's *Metamorphosis* human happiness was possible only through metamorphosing into the subhuman? 'All that saves them, like Philomela, is that they change into birds, beasts . . . Why can't they remain human?'

44

My question might have surprised Mr. Harrow, who sucked at his cigarillo for a moment, thoughtfully. Then he said, 'It's Ovid's judgment on the "human." There is no happiness in humanity, only in escaping strife. The ancient world was stoical, or you might say cynical. They didn't believe in anything like individual Christian redemption. Their gods were mean and vindictive as overgrown children.'

'But . . . there weren't any gods, really. They didn't believe in them, did they? *Really?*'

'The gods were passions. Obsessions. Appetites. So yes, they believed in these gods. They were terrified of them.'

Mr. Harrow glanced through several of my neatly typed poems. They were meticulously crafted Petrarchan sonnets. In the workshop the other poets had been awed and had offered little criticism; Mr. Harrow had himself praised the sonnets, and read one of them aloud. But now, to my dismay, it seemed he wasn't so impressed. 'Technically, your poetry is always interesting, Gillian, but . . .'— as if unconsciously he reached out to touch my wrist with his fingers, to comfort, console— '. . . unrealized. As if you'd trapped a butterfly in a cage and lavished all your effort into constructing the bars of the cage, and the butterfly is beating its wings to be released, and you've failed to see it.'

I knew. I knew this was so. I bit my lower

45

lip, and tried to keep the tears from spilling over onto my cheeks.

Lightly, Mr. Harrow squeezed my wrist.

He had more to say but someone rapped at the door behind me. I saw his attention shift, and an expression of annoyance cross his face. A senior named Michelle, long-legged and breathless, stood in the doorway staring at us. I scarcely knew Michelle, who was beautiful but pasty-skinned, very talented, with a reputation for being a druggie. 'Yes, Michelle? What do you want?'

'To see you, Andre. It's important.'

'Did we have an appointment?'

'Yes. We had an appointment.'

Michelle spoke sullenly as if to say *no we had no appointment but I'm here.* Uninvited she entered Mr. Harrow's office. She was smoking a cigarette. She'd scarcely glanced at me. I excused myself and left.

*   *   *

Unrealized.

At the edge of the playing fields I ran. On the spongy soil I ran at dusk. The soccer teams were gone, the air was still and cold. I ran pounding my heels like a young frenzied horse. In high school I'd been a gymnast, but I'd injured my back in a fall. My coach had pushed, pushed, pushed me. I had pushed, pushed, pushed myself. There'd been talk—

46

for a while—that I might be 'Olympic quality.' My father, who was frequently away on business, had made it a point to attend some of my matches; he'd been proud of me, or anyway he'd been proud when I won my matches. But I'd had to give up gymnastics. I was too small-boned for soccer, field hockey, basketball. The other, aggressive girls ran me over. And I hated competing, now. I ran alone in the early morning and often at dusk to breathe more deeply, to make my heart race, to cause myself some small tinge of pain. *Technically interesting but . . . unrealized.* On dirt paths through the woods I ran. Along Catamount Creek (where I'd followed Dorcas) I ran. The smell of pine needles! So sharp, tears sprang into my eyes and ran down my cheeks. *Unrealized!* Of course it was true. I'd known during our workshops, when the others offered their brief, somewhat baffled praise, that this was so. I'd known that Andre Harrow hadn't been truly impressed. I knew myself a failure. It was like falling from the bar, falling clumsily onto the mat, my back twisted, half-hoping it was broken. *Exactly what you deserve.*

Yet I felt the touch of his hand on my wrist, still.

I would sleep that night with my arm beside my head on the pillow. My face against my wrist. I would dream of the man with the kindly luminous face, the touch that, though

47

light, though in no way sexual or predatory, would suffuse my body with joy.

7. 'Philomela'

In Heath Cottage my friends teased me by calling me 'Philomela.' I think they meant no harm. I think they didn't hate me. Not Dominique with her olive-warm complexion and beautiful black eyes, not Marisa with her ashy hair and small, delicate features, not Penelope with her childlike, thick-lashed blue eyes that so easily welled with tears, not Sybil who so bit her nails, blood-droplets oozed at her fingertips, not Cassie with whom I felt most sisterly, the only girl I'd told about my parents' divorce . . . Maybe their mouths twisted just perceptibly. Maybe the name was drawn out ('Phil-o-melll-a') to make it sound ludicrous, shouted in the dining hall or outdoors.

Where's Phil-o-melll-a?
Upstairs?
Hell, who cares?

So I'd overhear. Sometimes. Not really often. These were my friends. I pressed my hands over my ears and hid in my room until they were safely gone.

I reread the tale of Philomela in Ovid's *Metamorphosis*. I hadn't realized how ugly it was. Philomela, a virgin, is brutally raped by a man who should have protected her, her brother-in-law Tereus; after he rapes her,

49

Tereus cuts out her tongue to prevent her accusing him. It's a typically Ovidian scene, vivid and cinematic and sadistic:

> The double drive of fear and anger drove
>   him
> To draw the sword, to catch her by the hair,
> To pull the head back, to tie the arms behind
>   her,
> And Philomela, at the sight of the blade,
> Was happy with hope, the thought of death
> Most welcome: her throat ready for the stroke.
> But Tereus did not kill her; he seized her
>   tongue
> With pincers, though it cried against the
>   outrage,
> Babbled and made a sound like *Father*,
> Till the sword cut it off. The mangled root
> quivered, the severed tongue along the
>   ground
> Lay quivering, making a little murmur,
> Jerking and twitching, the way a serpent
>   does . . .

But mute Philomela is no passive victim. With the aid of her loyal sister she takes bloody revenge on her rapist. And in the end she's metamorphosed into a bird with, as Mr. Harrow said approvingly, 'blood-colored' breast feathers.

A happy ending, then.
Is it?

8. *Brierly Lane*

OCTOBER 1975

She'd asked, *Which one of them are you?* meaning which one of Andre Harrow's students. I'd had no choice but to tell her my name.

Since that encounter in the Catamount post office I hadn't followed Dorcas. I knew she would see me, and recognize me. She might have waved at me. She might have laughed.

I regarded myself in my bureau mirror. Shirtless, my hard little breasts waxy-pale. My face in repose like a mask. My mother had often chided me when I was in high school for 'not trying' to be pretty like the other girls. I might have smiled more, I suppose. I might have smeared lipstick on my mouth.

Dreamily I took hold of my long, wavy, glinting hair in both hands and lifted it in thick strands and let it sift through my fingers slowly. I heard Dorcas's approving voice in my ear.

Très belle!

*　　　*　　　*

I made inquiries about Dorcas. I learned that from time to time Dorcas took a liking to a girl

51

and encouraged her husband to invite her to their house on Brierly Lane. These evenings involved delicious meals, and wine; intense conversations that lasted practically all night.

Sometimes a lucky girl was hired as Dorcas's intern. Sometimes, though rarely, a girl was invited to travel with Dorcas and Andre Harrow, who spent much of their summers in Europe.

It was rumored that, if you were so singled out by the Harrows, you had better not boast of it, nor even speak of it to your closest friends, or you'd never be invited back.

It was rumored that . . .

'No. People are just jealous. See, they don't get invited, they hear things, but they don't *know*. So they invent.' Dominique told me this derisively. Whenever she spoke of Andre Harrow lately, her voice took on a combative edge. Especially, she seemed resentful of me.

I told Dominique that Mr. Harrow had been severely critical of my poetry. I knew this would soften Dominique toward me, and so it did.

I asked Dominique if she knew of anyone who'd been invited to the Harrows and Dominique said quickly, 'No. I don't.'

I asked Dominique if she'd been invited, ever. She laughed, and lit one of her perpetual cigarettes. 'Absolutely no. *No*.'

I pointed out that, if she had been invited, she wouldn't tell me about it, would she?

I spoke wistfully, not at all accusingly. Dominique stroked my hair, and my shoulder; she squeezed my wrist in a way that reminded me uncomfortably of Andre Harrow. Her eyes were bloodshot from little sleep and too much caffeine; Dominique was generally an A-student, but one of those who procrastinated until, near the end of a semester, she was overwhelmed and frenzied by work. Her skin exuded heat, as if with fever. 'Why do you want to know, "Philo-mella"? What business is it of yours?'

But Dominique laughed to show me this was just teasing.

*   *   *

(In fact, according to Sybil, Dominique had been seen more than once walking on Brierly Lane after dark. She'd been seen in Andre Harrow's car in Great Barrington. And in the train depot in that city, waiting with Dorcas and Andre for the New York-bound train. When the poet John Berryman came to read at Catamount, at Andre Harrow's invitation, Dominique had been one of the few undergraduates invited to the party at Mr. Harrow's house afterward.)

*   *   *

At the rear of the old New England farmhouse

53

was a startlingly modern structure, an A-frame studio made mostly of glass. It was here that the sculptress Dorcas worked.

I knew the way to the house at 99 Brierly Lane, though I'd never been invited. I knew the stealthy back way.

Other faculty houses were scrupulously, fussily maintained, but not the house belonging to Dorcas and Andre Harrow. You could see that the inhabitants of 99 Brierly Lane were indifferent to appearances, for their house needed repainting, reshingling. Their front lawn was overgrown with juniper pines, birch, saplings.

It was the back way I knew best. Through the woods at the edge of campus. Like a sleepwalker I approached the house from the rear and stood in the dripping dark of pine trees, shivering . . . It was late. There was a glaring moon, but partly obscured by clouds. My teeth chattered. I believed myself, in the dark, in the woods behind the house, invisible to inhabitants within.

I had not wished to come here. Something had drawn me.

Something, someone . . . *Très belle.*

I'd come to about twenty feet behind the house. I could see, in Dorcas's studio, a number of tall, hulking figures, and in the foreground a moving figure. Dorcas was working late, making dreamy repetitive motions with both hands as if rubbing or

54

sanding a large surface. From where I crouched I couldn't see what she wore, or her face. But I could imagine her face.

And which one of them are you?

Gillian . . . My name is Gillian.

Gillian! Dorcas smiled. Her eyes shone with a curious sort of pleasure, you might almost mistake for mockery. *I like the name, so indépendant. Yes? You are?*

Yes. I think so.

Dorcas laughed again, gave my arm a squeeze, and walked away.

'Dorcas': a Greek name meaning 'girl of dark eyes.'

I'd been drawing nearer to the house. My legs were wet to the thighs. My heart was beating more calmly now, as if I'd been swimming against the current for some time but was now being borne by it, carried to shore.

Surreptitiously I'd made inquiries about Dorcas at the college. Under the pretense (except it wasn't pretense) of admiring her sculpted work and hoping to be one of her interns, someday. I'd learned that Dorcas and Andre Harrow had married in Paris in 1961; that Dorcas's mother had been an American and her father a mix of French, Hungarian, Greek.

I'd learned that Dorcas had been married before, that she was slightly older than Andre Harrow. Possibly, she had a child from her first

55

marriage, living now in Europe.

Dorcas and Andre Harrow had had no child together.

Mr. Harrow spoke of D. H. Lawrence as the great prophet of the twentieth century. Lawrence's god was the god of immediate physical sensation, a god to devastate all other gods. Lawrence saw the 'rotted edifice' of bourgeois/capitalist morality. *Where is the past? Where is the future? What exists for us except the present moment?*

We, Mr. Harrow's students, had no way of refuting such logic.

We believed, or wished to believe, it must be true.

Suddenly I saw—what?—another person in Dorcas's studio. Was it Andre Harrow? My heart leapt: I thought I recognized his hair, his beard. His way of carrying himself at a slight angle, with an air of deviousness, as if he looked at you sidelong. But, as I stared, I saw that there were two figures entering the studio. A man, and a girl or young woman. The man was Andre Harrow, the girl had ash-blond hair.

Marisa?

I tasted jealousy like bile. I saw how they moved together, the three. Like undersea figures. As a light was dimmed, as if a decision had been made. When I looked again the studio was darkened. There was nothing to see.

56

Where had they gone? (Upstairs?)

There was a single room lighted on the second floor.

I was very tired suddenly. My brain hurt; it teemed with impressions bright and fiercely scintillant as waves in a rushing stream. You put out your hands to cup the water, to slow its passage with your fingers . . . but you can't.

9. *False Alarm*

Not that night, but the following night, we were wakened in our beds in Heath Cottage by a deafening alarm.

Those of us who'd been sleeping were wakened. I was exhausted, I'd been sleeping heavily . . . Dominique had given me two of her prescription barbiturates: 'downers' she called them, fondly.

'Sometimes all you want is to be brought *down.* Way, way *down.* These will do the trick, Jill-y.'

Jill-y! Dominique had never called me that before.

And then at about four A.M. an alarm was pulled in Heath Cottage. Downstairs, in the corridor just beyond the mailboxes. It was our first false alarm in Heath Cottage. But we didn't know it was a false alarm, how could we have known? You stagger from bed dazed and panicked, groping for a coat, boots . . . you're so frightened your teeth are chattering, you're shivering convulsively even before you've run downstairs and outside into the cold.

Cassandra! Penelope! Dominique! Gillian!

Our names were being screamed by our resident advisor.

59

Cathy, Joan, Marisa . . . Where is Marisa?
We hugged one another, staggering like drunken girls. Of all of us in Heath Cottage, Dominique was the most flamboyant: the one with 'personality.' She hadn't undressed for bed. Her eyes were wide, wild. Cassie's face was whitely slick with complexion cream that smelled like Lysol. Penelope couldn't stop crying, though she was laughing, too.

'I mean, Christ . . . this is so ridiculous. There's no fire.'

'How d'you know?'

'You can smell a fire, for God's sake. Burning stuff *stinks*.'

The Catamount firetruck rushed to Heath Cottage but it was a fact, there turned out to be no fire for the disgruntled volunteers to extinguish. They were youngish guys, and unshaven. They stared at the girls of Heath Cottage as if we were naked. Only the chief was middle-aged, a tall, bald man with a megaphone voice. He was bossy, rude. He conferred with a security guard, a light-skinned black man whom we knew and liked, named Jonah. At about this time it began to rain.

A small crowd was gathering in the road near our residence, though it had been announced there'd be no fire tonight.

I wondered if, a half-mile away on Brierly Lane, Dorcas and Mr. Harrow had been wakened by the commotion. I hoped so.

60

And if anyone was with them, I hoped she'd been wakened, too.

The firemen were leaving. There'd been a few smiles exchanged. Somehow we knew the firemen were all married; local men married young and had children immediately. Dominique had bummed a cigarette from one of the firemen and was smoking in the rain. She said, 'It's weird. I feel like dancing! Who can go to bed, after this?'

'Yeah. You feel kind of let down, with no fire.'

'Are you two crazy? You don't want a fire!'

'No. But . . .'

Marisa was sullen and puffy-faced, rudely awakened from sleep. She'd joined us, shivering in the sheepskin jacket her Dartmouth boyfriend had given her.

'This is so *unfair.* I have a biology exam at ten tomorrow. One more time, and I'm going to transfer out of this fucking college.'

'Marisa, where were you?'

'What? Where was *I*? Where were *you*?'

*   *   *

Next day we were questioned, one by one, by the dean of students and the head of campus security. We, the twelve residents of Heath Cottage. Heath was the smallest residence in which a false alarm had been set off and so there was the reasonable assumption that the

61

guilty party might be identified. She might be emotionally disturbed, she might impulsively confess.

I was never a serious suspect, I think. The resident advisor had seen how groggy I'd been, staggering downstairs. I'd been white-faced with shock, the barbiturate sleep had been so heavy.

Cassie, who'd signed up for psychological counselling in September, complained bitterly of being singled out for protracted questioning. We were incensed on her behalf. It was so unfair! Catamount College was always urging its high-strung students to 'seek out counselling' if they were having emotional problems; then, if they did, they were suspected of deviant behavior.

I thought, *I will never make that mistake. Not me!*

The day following the false alarm I felt like a zombie. My throat was parched, I kept swallowing compulsively. My eyes were dry, tearless. In my classes I drifted off while my professors lectured. I would tell Dominique, *No more downers.*

Dominique (who, like other Catamount girls, had a cache of pills for every occasion) offered me a bennie—Benzedrine?—to elevate my spirits. Adamantly I told her, *No thanks!* I wanted to face what's called reality with my eyes open.

I've made that a principle for my life.

Sometimes I wonder if this has been a wise decision.

The guilty party was never located in Heath Cottage. Either she was a brilliant liar, or she wasn't a resident of Heath Cottage after all. And no one impulsively confessed. It was argued by our resident advisor, a young woman not much older than we were, that someone from another residence might have entered Heath and hidden until after hours, then set the alarm, and fled. There were always numerous people coming and going. Friends visiting friends, including guys from Amherst, Williams, U. Mass. The front door wasn't locked until midnight. And sometimes even at midnight it wasn't locked. We were always being scolded for our carelessness about security . . .

I said, exasperated, 'It would almost be a relief, wouldn't it?—if one of us was caught, or confessed.'

By the way in which they looked at me I understood that I'd blurted out something very wrong. I'd said something no one else would have wished to say.

10. The Kiss

It was purely chance, our meeting. Mr. Harrow would have believed so.

That November afternoon, dusk shading into night, when Andre Harrow kissed me for the first time.

I'd felt bold, nervy. I thought, *Why can't I be Dominique, just this once?*

We met, we fell into stride together, on the snowy path behind the library. Evergreen boughs were heavy with snow, our breaths steamed in the freezing air. This was romance!

'Gillian? I thought that was you.'

'Mr. Harrow. Hello.'

There was Professor Andre Harrow walking briskly and carrying a briefcase, in a slim, navy jacket, a black astrakhan hat on his head. He hesitated, seeing me. Then he smiled, baring his teeth. I shivered as if he'd drawn those teeth over me.

The chapel bell began to toll the half-hour. Five-thirty P.M.

In the Berkshires, in this season, dusk comes early. Rising like a dark tide out of the earth.

In our workshop that morning Mr. Harrow had been less patient with us than usual. He'd

65

prodded dull asthmatic Catherine nearly to tears. He had praise, to a degree, for Dominique; but not for the rest of us. We felt the sting of his lash. We winced, and bit our lips to keep from crying, knowing he was right.

' "The blood-jet is poetry." *Go for the jugular.*'

Now by chance we'd met, we were walking together on the snowy path behind the library. In the direction of the playing fields, and the woods. Catamount Creek was now frozen over. The scent of pine needles was sharper than ever.

We were talking. Mr. Harrow was talking. His mood was never predictable and now it seemed he was enlivened, invigorated, smiling sidelong at me as if he wasn't certain exactly who I was, or what I meant. And I was feeling nervy, giddy. Thinking why couldn't I be Dominique, for just a brief while?

I envied my beautiful friend's olive-dark complexion, her warm, wet eyes, her husky laugh, and full, fleshy lips.

Lips made for kissing. Lips made to be kissed.

The chapel bell. A beautiful sound but melancholy.

Cassie confided in me, she'd signed up for psychological counseling because she had 'troubled thoughts,' 'racing thoughts,' 'thoughts about ways to hurt myself.' I hugged her, and told her it was all right.

But was it? What exactly was *all right*?

It was twelve days since the false fire alarm. There had been no further alarms, genuine or false, since that night.

Sybil was in the infirmary. Or, maybe, she'd gone home to be sick. Mononucleosis? Hepatitis? We made inquires, we were concerned for our friend, but no one would tell us except Sybil would be missing classes through Thanksgiving.

Mr. Harrow, seeing that Sybil was absent from the workshop, merely frowned. It was rare that our professor would comment on any of us when we weren't present; we interpreted this as a sign of tact.

In fact, when Marisa reported that Sybil would probably be absent until after Thanksgiving, Mr. Harrow thanked her for the information but said nothing more.

Later he told us, 'There's one cardinal rule of my workshops: I want only not to be bored shitless by you.'

In love at a distance, so much has to be invented.

I wondered: was Dominique reclaiming Mr. Harrow this semester? Did Dorcas know? Was there a triangle of Dorcas, Andre Harrow, and twenty-year-old Dominique Landau? But there was Michelle: pasty-faced Michelle. I'd seen the look that had passed between her and Mr. Harrow. And there was Marisa.

In our workshops Marisa was a strong

67

presence, too. There were times when Marisa seemed to me more beautiful, or in any case more fascinating, than Dominique. The two competed for Mr. Harrow's favor. (But I was no longer so certain I'd seen Marisa in Dorcas's studio that night. I'd had a glimpse only of a girl or a young woman with ashy-blond hair; I hadn't seen her face. The lights in the studio were so quickly dimmed. The figures so quickly departed. Going where? Upstairs to the bedroom?)

Mr. Harrow was walking with me at the edge of campus. Overhead the sky was tattered, windblown clouds, illuminated intermittently by the moon. Staring at it you felt as if you were staring into a swiftly moving dark stream in which broken light was reflected. Mr. Harrow's arm, his gloved hand, brushed against my arm. At one point the path was icy, I began to slip, he caught me and steadied me. He said, 'Gillian, you're such a little girl. You must weigh eighty-nine pounds.'

I laughed, embarrassed. I thought of Dorcas's firm, voluptuous flesh.

'It isn't evident from your poetry if you have a lover. Lovers? You're maddeningly circumspect.'

With a throaty Dominique laugh I said, 'But I thought that was what poetry is, Mr. Harrow: circumspect. If it wasn't, it would just be *talk*.'

'That's very well put, Gillian. You always put things so very well.'

68

I must have imagined it: a faint smell of wine? whiskey? on Mr. Harrow's breath. And the musky smell of the Dutch cigarillo that didn't dissipate even in the open air.

We were walking at the edge of the woods. No one was around. In the distance, girls' voices, laughter. Mr. Harrow spoke of the great modernist visionaries. Yeats, Joyce, Lawrence. The apocalyptic ending of Lawrence's *The Rainbow* in which the pregnant Ursula is menaced by a herd of magnificent horses. What is merely human in her is extirpated by the beasts; she's freed of her human ties, and the rainbow appears to her as a vision of transformation. Reading this extraordinary prose I'd been deeply moved. I'd imagined myself Ursula, though I knew I lacked the young woman's ferocity of will. Mr. Harrow was saying, 'The wisdom of Lawrence, as of the ancients, is simply this: you can't deny Eros. You can't resist Eros. Eros will strike, like lightning. Our human defenses are frail, ludicrous. Like plasterboard houses in a hurricane. Your triumph is in perfect submission. And the god of Eros will flow through you, as Lawrence says, in the "perfect obliteration of bloodconsciousness." '

My cheeks were smarting with cold. I was aware of Mr. Harrow as a man, a physical presence. We were alone, I was frightened suddenly and tried to think: What would Dominique do? What were the things

Dominique did, with Andre Harrow? I understood that I'd crossed a line. I'd blundered over a line. By accompanying this man, who might have been any man, in this way, out of the lighted area of the campus and into the dark where there were only intermittent lights on poles to guide our way, I was behaving like fierce, passionate Ursula of *The Rainbow*, but I was not Ursula, I was not Dominique, I was Gillian.

Mr. Harrow had asked about a lover. Lovers.

The boys I knew were intellectual, high-strung, bookish like me. To the extent to which a guy's skin is blemished, he inclines to irony. Even when not stricken by physical shyness my boyfriends lacked the ease of experience. Sometimes they attempted an eager, awkward sort of lovemaking, but they were not 'lovers.' Mostly we talked. We knew too much, yet not enough.

And always in my imagination there was the figure of Andre Harrow looming between me and any boy. *Don't be afraid,* Mr. Harrow urged me in my poetry.

Go deeper!

Go for the jugular.

Suddenly he was kissing me. He was gripping my shoulders and pressing his mouth, that tasted of tobacco, and of something else, against mine. It wasn't a kiss, it was purely pressure. A stinging kiss. A biting kiss. There

70

was haste in it, and anger. I stumbled, I pushed dazedly at the man. We were—where? Not so far from the campus as I'd believed but behind a darkened storage building. Down behind the tennis courts. There was a man looming over me, excited, impatient, forcing my mouth open, trying to insert his tongue into my mouth, but I panicked, and resisted. I was too confused to respond. It was an animal reaction, unthinking. As if I'd forgotten that this man, finally touching me as I'd yearned for him to do for months, was Andre Harrow . . .

A wave of dizziness rose sharply in me and there was Mr. Harrow holding me upright by my arm, and not gently. 'Gillian? Hey, I was only joking.'

He was furious. But amused. He was mature enough to be amused. Firmly he gripped my elbow, steering me back toward campus. He would be protective now. He would be brisk, brusque now. He would provide the narration, the interpretation, for what had happened, as, in his lectures and workshops, he controlled such information.

'We had an unfortunate misunderstanding, Gillian. Nothing more.'

As if he'd struck me a blow instead of kissed me.

11. The Departed

Sybil wouldn't be returning after Thanksgiving after all.

One Sunday evening we tried to call her. There were five of us, we intended to take turns on the phone. Mainly, we wanted to tell Sybil we missed her. In Heath Cottage, and in our poetry workshop.

We would tell her that Mr. Harrow missed her, too.

Though he hadn't said a word about her. Though he'd removed the eleventh chair from our seminar table, and set it in a corner of the room. The other chairs were spread out evenly around the table so that you'd swear no one was missing.

Sybil's mother answered the phone. They lived in a suburb of Providence, Rhode Island; of the five of us, only Cassie had visited Sybil at home. Mrs. Merchant, Sybil's mother, told us that Sybil couldn't come to the telephone, who was calling, please? It made Sybil seem so young to us, that her mother was speaking for her, protecting her. We said, 'We miss Sybil. We . . . miss her a lot. Is she O.K.?' It was an awkward question. We knew that Sybil wasn't O.K. Quickly Mrs. Merchant said that Sybil

73

was fine, Sybil was doing very well but tired easily, and couldn't talk with us just then. She had a reedy, nasal voice. She might have been upset with us and trying to be polite. We wanted to leave a message for Sybil but Mrs. Merchant interrupted: 'Write to my daughter, please. Don't telephone again. I'm sorry, I'm going to hang up now.'

* * *

What was wrong with Sybil, why was it a secret? No one in Heath Cottage seemed to know. Of course, there were theories.

One night when the chapel bell was tolling the hour of eleven, Cassie began to shiver. 'That bell! Sybil said it scared her, it was so beautiful late at night. But also sad. Like it reminded her of . . .' Cassie paused delicately, seeking the right word. Not a crass word. *Death, dying. Suicide?*

I was frightened suddenly. I asked, 'Did Sybil try to kill herself?'

Cassie's face shut up like a fist. Stiffly she said, 'Sorry, Gillian. I can't betray Sybil's confidence even to *you*.'

* * *

(I lay awake trying to decipher what Cassie meant by so emphasizing *you*. Did it mean that Cassie wouldn't betray her friend Sybil even with me, who was a closer friend to her than Sybil; or, did it mean that Cassie wouldn't betray Sybil even with me, who so resembled Sybil? And, if so, *in what way did I resemble Sybil?*)

* * *

Shortly after this, Sybil's mother and an older married sister drove to Catamount from Providence to pack Sybil's things and clear out her room. I was surprised: Mrs. Merchant was nearly my mother's age, an exhausted-looking woman in her fifties. Or maybe it was grief that had aged her. She was polite to us but restrained in her speech. When we asked how Sybil was she said, 'Fine. Sybil is fine.' Upstairs I introduced myself and offered to help them pack Sybil's things. I saw Mrs. Merchant and her older daughter hesitate, exchange glances. Mrs. Merchant said, 'That would be kind . . .'

Her mouth moved numbly, already she'd forgotten my name.

I was put in charge of packing Sybil's papers and books. Clearing out her desk drawers. I had a certain predilection for neatness, for arranging things in files, so this worked out well. I hoped I might discover poems of Sybil's, or a journal, something she'd never presented to the workshop, but she must have taken such private material home with her, or destroyed it.

I found only, at the bottom of a drawer into

75

which geology, Intro to Anthropology, and German II notes had been dumped, a single Polaroid of Sybil posed before a life-sized wooden figure of a primitive female. One of Dorcas's totems! It was one I recognized, from last spring's exhibit. Where the figure's arms were akimbo, Sybil's arms were akimbo; where the figure's head was thrown back, Sybil's head was thrown back. Sybil had been posed, but playfully. She looked drunk, or high. Her dark, disheveled hair was trimmed short, which meant that the Polaroid had been taken earlier this semester; last year, Sybil had worn her hair long. I saw that she was a wanly pretty girl with a petulant expression. Her lips seemed always pursed, as for a kiss. The snapshot wasn't very flattering for Sybil had blinked at the wrong moment. She was wearing one of her flimsy Indian skirts, and apparently nothing beneath; you could see a shadowy triangle at the fork of her slender legs. Her blouse, too, was made of see-through material. She had sizable breasts, with dark nipples like tiny eyes. I slipped the Polaroid into my pocket without being seen; I would examine it in private, many times.

It must have been taken in Dorcas's studio. I wondered who'd taken it.

12. 'Anatomical Specimens'

Don't be fearful: excavate your soul.
  Go deeper!
You can't go deeper? Go deeper.
Go for the jugular.
  But I could not. Alone of Mr. Harrow's students, I could not seem to follow his instructions.
  For now we were keeping journals, and reading excerpts at the start of each workshop. Mr. Harrow had lost patience with our attempts at poetry. Like a father disappointed with his children yet emotionally bound to them, unwilling to give up on them, Mr. Harrow insisted that we keep 'intimate, honest' journals preparatory to writing our poetry. He wanted 'no lies, no subterfuge, no "nice-girl" bullshit.' We were to record our dreams, our fantasies, our hopes, our visions; our personal relationships with parents, siblings, friends, lovers; we were to examine our emotional, physical, sexual lives as if we were 'anatomical specimens.'
  If we wanted to be writers we must examine the world with fresh, skeptical eyes.
  Especially, Mr. Harrow warned us against the dangers of self-censorship, 'self-castration.'

Dominique impudently asked, 'Andre? Technically speaking, can women be castrated?'

Mr. Harrow said, 'Dear girl, women *are* castrated. You must struggle to reverse your pitiable condition.'

We laughed, laughed. But Mr. Harrow wasn't smiling.

*　　　*　　　*

Since the 'misunderstanding' between Mr. Harrow and me, I knew myself isolated in the workshop. My fragile little boat was being buffeted about, rudderless. Mr. Harrow was coolly polite to me. If he smiled, his smile was ironic. He no longer teased me by calling me 'Philomela'—he didn't call me 'Gillian,' either. He never turned to me to ask my opinion about anything. I was naive enough to think that he regretted what had happened, as I did; I was slow to comprehend that he was furious with me, and would have to be placated.

He was the father who withholds his love, with devastating results.

I thought of Sybil. Listening to the bell tolling the hour, the quarter-hour, the half-hour. Through the night. I wondered how many Catamount students lay awake listening to that melancholy yet reassuring sound. *There is a way out. You know the way out.*

I wondered what method Sybil had tried. If she'd tried to slash her wrists, we would have known. A drug overdose? I tried to recall the circumstances of Sybil leaving Heath Cottage, the last time I'd seen her, but I could not.

Andre Harrow might know. Dorcas might know.

Strange how, in our workshop, my friends must have noticed how Mr. Harrow's attitude changed toward me, overnight. Yet no one said a word.

He ignored me, mostly. But when he couldn't ignore me, his praise was subtly jeering: '*Very* well done. A crossword puzzle of a poem, eh?'

The others, sensing my vulnerability, sprang to the attack. Had they been jealous of me, resentful of me, for months? Sonnets, sestinas! Complex slant-rhymes! I was shocked and hurt that Penelope, who'd always said she admired my poetry, was disdainful now. 'A poem isn't supposed to be a crossword puzzle, is it? A poem should *sing.*' With a pose of reluctance Dominique said that she thought it was 'supremely cool' how Gillian rhymed the 'weirdest' words—'You always learn something from her poems, that's for sure, looking words up in the dictionary'—but, in the end, 'I have to say: *who cares?*' Marisa shook her cottony hair and frowned as if my poetry were a puzzle too demanding to be solved any longer. There was sniffy Catherine, and there was Robin . . . I listened in silence. I wanted only to rush from the room, humiliated, but I wouldn't give them the satisfaction.

What did I care for these girls' opinions, I cared only for Andre Harrow's opinion. I loved him, still.

*   *   *

' "A journal is an ax for the frozen sea within" '—so Mr. Harrow paraphrased Kafka. 'But it must be truthful. Unsparing.'

We began to be obsessed with journal-keeping. Some of us began to neglect our other courses. The poetry workshop with Andre Harrow met for longer than its scheduled two hours, often longer than three hours, at the end of which we were exhausted; meetings were on Tuesdays and Fridays, and our lives began to revolve around them. The atmosphere was tense, taut. There was no professor like Andre Harrow to listen so closely, so attentively, to us. Some of us read in forceful, self-dramatizing voices; some of us read quietly, shyly. Sometimes Mr. Harrow interrupted with an exclamation—'Beautiful,' or, 'Again, please. Reread.' But often he was disappointed. As he inelegantly phrased it, 'Pissed.' He brought his fist down hard on the seminar table, shaking our Styrofoam coffee cups and our pens, as if he'd been personally insulted.

That an adult man, a professor, should care so much for the quality of undergraduate

80

women's work . . . This seemed to us not strange and troubling, but wonderful. Or, if strange and troubling, it was wonderful, still.

Only care for me. If you can't love me. Only don't ignore me . . .

Others in the workshop were inspired by the new assignment, and were doing better work. At least, Mr. Harrow judged it better work. Dominique, Penelope, and Marisa had quickly emerged in the workshop as rivals. Their poetry was amateurish, formless, but their journal entries were often riveting. They'd followed Mr. Harrow's instruction to record without 'self-censorship.' Candidly they wrote of intimate secrets. There was a focus upon childhood, traumatic and demeaning memories. Initial sexual experiences, anxieties. They described their own bodies, what they liked about them and what they hated; they described others' bodies, parents, lovers, in graphic detail. They described lurid, violent sexual fantasies and sexual acts. They outdid one another describing menstruation. Dominique excelled in manic-lyric, 'acid-dropping' flights. (Those weekends at Dartmouth and Williams . . .) But we were most astonished to learn that Dominique was of, what she called, 'brown' Barbadoan ancestry: her mother's family was from Barbados, there was 'mixed blood' somewhere, so Dominique considered herself 'a light-skinned black' who 'really grooved' on fucking white guys. 'I mean, like it really turns me on, like I'm thinking, does this guy know who I *am*?' Dominique's parents were divorcing, she'd just been informed, but this was good news, because her father was an alcoholic and had long been abusive of the family; he'd cracked Dominique's eardrum when she was six and sent her mother to the emergency room more than once. He was a 'big-deal corporate attorney' with a cruel, sadistic streak. In related stream-of-consciousness poems Dominique hinted of sexual abuse . . . Mr. Harrow was impressed. If he'd praised Dominique before, he really praised Dominique now. 'This is the material of nightmare, therefore the material of potentially great art.'

Penelope, too, had had a troubled childhood. Her father also drank, and her mother had tried to commit suicide several times, though always it was hushed up— ' "messy things don't happen in Cincinnati," my grandmother says.' Penelope was made to attend a private girls' school where there were 'just debutantes' but one day she came home to discover her mother naked and unconscious on her bathroom floor, bleeding from slashed wrists . . . 'I was fifteen. She'd tried this before. I just looked at her. I thought: Should I call an ambulance, or shut the door and pretend I hadn't seen her?' Penelope read her excerpt in a tremulous, thrilled voice. We were riveted by her. A soft-seeming, sweetly funny girl most of the time, a solid B+ student in most of her courses, with a fair, sensitive skin that broke out when she was nervous (she was nervous now: there was a rash like sunburn across her forehead), she'd been a closer friend during our freshman year; I'd always admired Penelope for her solid good sense and reliability. Now she was saying, 'I made my decision: I called 911. Sure! My mother was manipulating me like a puppet. *I am a puppet in others' hands.*' She looked up, seeing how we were staring at her; her childlike blue eyes brimmed with tears of conviction and righteousness. 'But, if I'm a puppet, I intend to choose who will be my master. *From now on.*'

Penelope's lower lip trembled. I saw how she yearned to glance at Andre Harrow, at the farther end of the seminar table, who was staring avidly at her. But she resisted.

Mr. Harrow said, 'Very well done, Penelope! That's powerful material for poetry. Like Greek myth. This *is* the jugular.'

Yet over a half-dozen of these sessions, Marisa was emerging as the star. As she read from her journal she smoked, in airy, self-dramatizing puffs; she'd been taking dance lessons since the age of four, and several times she rose from her seat and moved about dreamily as she read or recited her excerpts. Marisa captivated our attention: a fragile, doll-like girl with a mane of ash-blond hair and

83

a beautiful heart-shaped face who might have been fourteen, not twenty. Even in the bitter cold of a Berkshires winter Marisa often wore flimsy skirts and blouses; the skirts were layered wraparounds that fell to her ankles, the blouses were often low-cut so that we could see how painfully thin Marisa had become in the past several months, how prominent her collar bone and small creamy-pale breasts. Marisa seemed to have shocked even Mr. Harrow with her graphic and unsparing description of having been sexually abused by an older male cousin when she was eight. There'd been a 'trusted family friend' and also a 'much-beloved grade school teacher' who'd continued this abuse for years. When Marisa was twelve, though, she'd had her first 'freely chosen lover'—a high school senior. Though unknowing that Marisa was sexually active, her mother had put her on the pill 'practically before' her first period at age thirteen. (Marisa was the daughter of a highly successful ABC-TV producer and his former-actress wife; they lived in Westchester County, not many miles from my home. But Marisa hadn't been a very close friend of mine at Catamount.) Now, Marisa informed us, she was in love with X. 'Well,' Marisa said provocatively, brushing her hair out of her eyes and glancing across the table at Mr. Harrow, '—also Y, and Z.' She'd only recently met Z—an 'older man, thirty-two'—

84

who lived in Manhattan and worked in a gallery; when her parents believed she was spending the weekend at, for instance, Yale, she was likely to be in New York in Z's loft 'getting high. And I mean *high*.' She was concerned, though, that Z might be bisexual; she'd witnessed a 'big, beautiful, black Jamaican' practically stick his hands in Z's trousers at a party . . . She was having flashes after some of these parties, like her head was going to explode. Sometimes voices whispered to her mean, malicious things; crazy things like 'set yourself on fire.' Sometimes food made her nauseated, especially breakfast; she'd rush away and stick a finger down her throat and puke everything up and what a 'rush' that was, how good it felt . . .

Mr. Harrow was deeply impressed with Marisa's performance. It was difficult for the rest of us not to feel a pang of jealousy, seeing the expression in his face. Though Marisa sometimes looked ravaged, emaciated. Though her bluish eyelids twitched. 'Very good. Very dramatic. You've certainly gone for the jugular here, Marisa.' Mr. Harrow seemed to have no interest in Marisa's physical symptoms but to be most intrigued by her lover Z. 'The dessicated old categories of "male" and "female" need to be destroyed. "Bisexual" identity is the future. It's the most challenging of discoveries because it confounds what society wants us to accept as "normal." The tyranny of the "normal"!'

Mr. Harrow made a spitting gesture, pronouncing 'normal.'

After one of Marisa's excerpts Mr. Harrow recited for us a poem by D. H. Lawrence containing these sensuous seductive lines:

I love you, rotten,
Delicious rottenness.

I love to suck you out from your skins
So brown and soft and coming suave,
So morbid . . .

Sorb-apples, medlars with dead crowns.
I say, wonderful are the hellish experiences,
Orphic, delicate
Dionysos of the Underworld.

A kiss, and a spasm of farewell, a moment's
  orgasm of rupture,
Then along the damp road alone, till the
  next turning.
And there, a new partner, a new parting . . .
A new intoxication of loneliness, among
  decaying, frost-cold leaves.

I shut my eyes. I wanted to cry. I had never heard so beautiful a poem, in so beautiful a male voice.

13. The Late Birth

NOVEMBER 1975

You can't go deeper? Go deeper.
Go for the jugular.
I remember the chapel bell tolling. I remember the arctic glisten to the snow-crust. And how sharp the snow-crust was, brittle as frosted glass. Nights were the challenge. Like Sybil sometimes wanting to hurt herself. Like Marisa hearing mean malicious seductive voices. *Fire. Fire. The jugular. Go for it!* My eyelids drooped and I saw my friend Penelope pushing open a door, staring down in horror at a body lying in a pool of blood on the floor. (But who was this body, was it me?) Since her revelation about her 'brown' background Dominique was conspicuously avoiding us. It hurt me most because I'd been (I thought) Dominique's special friend in Heath Cottage.

Before the tension in our workshop, Dominique and I had shown each other all our poetry. We'd read our work aloud. I missed her.

And yet: it was Andre Harrow I wished desperately to please. If I could please him, I reasoned, I'd be safe. No one could harm me.

Not even myself.

Gradually my other professors faded in significance. I began to cut classes. I was too restless to sit through a boring lecture. In the college chapel I was too restless to sit and had to pace about; if others were there, trying to pray or meditate, I annoyed them; they asked me please to leave.

I hadn't gone home over Thanksgiving break, and would not go home at Christmas. My parents were divorced. Well, I'd 'divorced' them.

I rarely thought of them. Rarely dreamt of them. They were ceasing to exist to me. As Andre Harrow, so conspicuously withdrawing from me, loomed larger and larger.

Don't be fearful: excavate your soul.

How obsession begins, takes root like a virulent weed . . .

Cassie suggested that I come with her to the Psych Center as it was called. I laughed, I told her no thanks—'My thoughts are my own private business.'

Who wants her thoughts recorded in a computer bank? For anyone to discover? Who wants to be known as a patient? Seeing a therapist? A shrink?

You'd be one of the first suspects. When/if a catastrophe occurred.

I wanted desperately to please Andre Harrow, but I could not. I tried, I tried, but I could not.

I believed that Mr. Harrow would forgive me, if my work improved. I accepted that he would never love me; how ridiculous to have fantasized such a possibility. He had Dorcas, and he had others. But he'd always seemed to admire my work, even to be impressed by it. Thoughtfully he'd said, now it seemed a long time ago, 'Yours is the art of indirection and ellipsis, Gillian. Yours is the art that can grow.'

Yet he'd lost patience with that art. It was another kind, direct as a Polaroid shot, confrontational, confessional, Mr. Harrow wanted now. *Go deeper. Deeper.* I wrote for hours in my journal, late at night. And I hated everything I wrote. I hated 'confessing'—I hated exposing myself in this way. And I knew myself inadequate. My thin body set beside Dominique's voluptuous body. My quiet manner set beside Marisa's exhibitionism. Even more, I didn't want to betray the secrets of others. I respected my parents, I guess I felt sorry for them even if, as I thought, I no longer loved them. It would be cruel to expose them to strangers . . . *And do I know them? How do I know them, except as their daughter born when they were middle-aged?*

When Mr. Harrow first encouraged us to write about our parents, including the sexual

89

lives of our parents, I'd been astonished to think that, yes of course, my parents had sexual lives. Not only with each other but before they'd met. My mother, a matronly woman obsessed with her household and with a close circle of women friends, an unimaginative woman I'd always thought her, had had her romances . . . of whom one had been my father.

My father! It was difficult to believe he'd ever been young. Always he'd seemed to me middle-aged. He had a heavy, handsome face, a dissatisfied mouth, dents in his flesh. He was exquisitely polite even with my mother and me: a way of avoidance. His smile was unconvincing, the smile of a man who knows that something he should have foreseen will shortly go wrong.

At first I'd thought that my father must have left my mother for another woman but the sadder truth was, he'd simply left.

To imagine them without clothes, to imagine them making love was not possible.

Only one significant memory came to me. I wondered what Mr. Harrow would make of it.

I am a late birth. Born when my mother was forty-one. When my father was in his early fifties. My birth was a 'miracle'—no one had expected it. Miracles are unnatural.

Yet in another sense I'd been born too early. I was only eight years old when John F. Kennedy was assassinated in November 1963.

I'd been too young to be aware of, much less involved in, the political turmoil of the sixties. The great revolution of the American twentieth century. My parents never spoke of the Vietnam War. They never spoke of the demonstrations against the war. They never spoke of the changes that were taking place beyond the boundaries of our three-acre property in northern Westchester County, New York. Which assassination had it been?— Martin Luther King, Jr.'s?—my parents had been baffled, embarrassed, apologetic in the presence of our black housekeeper, Nella, who'd insisted upon coming to work on the day of King's funeral. I remember my mother saying weakly, 'Nella, you may go home if you wish. You may take the day off.' She'd felt it necessary to add, in a lowered voice, 'You'll be paid.' But Nella refused. In the kitchen she'd cooked, and wept. I'd heard deep guttural sobs. I'd felt the tension in the air of our usually sedate household, and at dinner I saw my parents glancing guiltily at each other. Yet they were also baffled and resentful, as Caucasians of their class and time. *What have we to do with that woman's emotions? What is this grief we can't share?* In this, my mother and father understood each other completely.

When, next morning, I reread what I'd written, I tore it up in disgust.

'I can't. I can't betray them.'

14. *The Surrender*

NOVEMBER 1975

With cold-chafed knuckles I rapped on Andre Harrow's office door, making a sharper noise than I'd intended. The Humanities Building was nearly deserted but I knew that Mr. Harrow was inside his office: I heard voices.

Lights were on inside. But the window in the door was frosted, opaque.

It was a Monday afternoon, as dark outside as night. Snow falling in wet clumps. I heard the chapel bell ringing: five-fifteen.

Andre Harrow, who never appeared on the Catamount campus before two in the afternoon, often stayed late in his office, seeing students. He came now to the door to open it and when he saw who I was, he made no pretense of welcome.

'You? You don't have an appointment.'

'I'll wait.'

The unexpected edge in my voice caught Andre Harrow's attention. He smiled at me quizzically. He was wearing a coarse-knit olive-green sweater over a rumpled flannel shirt and he looked unshaven. At our last workshop, the previous Friday, he hadn't glanced at me once. He said now, indifferently, 'But I'm leaving after this conference. Sorry.'

'No. I'll wait.'

From Heath Cottage a quarter-mile away I'd run bareheaded, gloveless. I waited in the corridor outside Mr. Harrow's office, which was semidarkened. I was too restless to sit, I paced about in a looping figure eight. *Sorry!* he'd said. I mouthed the word like a hurt, furious child.

I told myself I couldn't bear another long weekend like the one I'd just endured.

Snowflakes were melting in my windblown hair and on my heated cheeks. I was terrified, but elated. I recalled Mr. Harrow's hard, punishing kiss and the grip of his fingers on my shoulders. I wanted only for him to forgive me: to touch me. In tenderness or in hurt, simply to touch me. It would be no worse (I told myself) than slipping from the bar. The graceful girl gymnast suddenly losing control, falling, landing heavily on her legs and lower back. That hushed moment when the crowd, having anticipated an occasion for applause, realizes it won't be applauding after all.

Daddy, I'm sorry.

Daddy, I'm so ashamed.

It was poor Catherine from the poetry workshop who'd come to speak with Mr. Harrow. A girl with wide, soft hips and pink, rabbity face, biting her lips to keep from crying. *You, too, unloved. Unlovely.* Mr. Harrow got rid of Catherine but didn't open the door fully, to invite me inside.

94

I knocked boldly on the part-opened door and Mr. Harrow, waiting for me, seeing the expression in my face, the dilated eyes, the look of raw yearning, knew why I'd come. He was wholly in control. 'May I come inside, Mr. Harrow?' I asked. He said, 'Sure. But not to discuss your schoolgirl poetry.' He moved swiftly behind me to glance out into the corridor, where no one was waiting. He shut the door and turned the lock. He switched off the overhead light; the crook-necked lamp on his desk remained on.

Always I would remember: that warm, intense penumbra of light in Andre Harrow's shadowy office.

Always I would remember: the cigarillo burning in an ashtray. That acrid smell making my eyes water.

Mr. Harrow told me to remove my coat and I obeyed, numbly. He stroked my hair, and framed my face with his hands, his big thumbs stretching the skin at the corner of my eyes. 'I like your nerve, Gillian. I'm impressed.' He bent to kiss me, lightly. His eyes were open, bemused. 'You're trembling like a trapped bird. I like that, too.' He opened a filing cabinet drawer and took out a bottle of wine; he poured wine into two coffee mugs, and passed one to me, to lift to my mouth. I was trembling so badly, I was so excited, I had to steady the cup with both hands.

'Who knows you're here?'

95

I shook my head wordlessly. No one knew.

He laughed. He was very happy suddenly. 'Your problem, "Philomela," is you talk too much.'

'Mr. H-Harrow—'

'"Andre," for Christ's sake. Call me "Andre."'

'"Andre." I—love you.'

Mr. Harrow laughed again. He drank the remainder of his wine as one might drink coffee, and took my cup from me. He pushed me onto my knees; onto a braided rug laid upon the hardwood floor. His hand at the nape of my neck was unhesitating.

'I've been waiting for you, girl, for a long time.'

* * *

When we left the darkened Humanities Building it was sometime after seven. I'd heard the chapel bell. I was dazed and disoriented. The wine had made me laugh like a frightened child but now the wine was making my head ache. Mr. Harrow had sent me to the women's restroom on the first floor to 'fix yourself up.' In the mirror, my eyes failed to come into focus. My mouth was bruised. I'd vowed to Andre Harrow that I loved him, I loved him and I would die for him, and he'd laughed at these extravagant words and asked what good would I be to him then, a dead girl. And in the

96

lavatory mirror there floated the waxy-pale face of the dead girl. Her bruised, aching mouth.

'But I do. You'll see. *I love you.*'

When we left the darkened Humanities Building, it seemed that a long time must have passed. I stumbled on the snowy steps and Mr. Harrow steadied me and when I turned in the direction of the upper quadrangle, and the residence in which I lived, he stopped me. 'But—where are we going?'

Mr. Harrow said, 'Dorcas has been waiting for you, too.'

15. The Fire

DECEMBER 1975

I wasn't a witness to any of it. I'd been nowhere near.

When fire alarms went off in Heath House. Smoke detectors in the basement laundry room. Screams and hysteria. Drew Weldon crying for help, her hands bleeding where the razor had cut her.

'Marisa? It was—*Marisa*?'

Local newspapers would eagerly report: CATAMOUNT COLLEGE ARSONIST TAKEN INTO CUSTODY.

And, CATAMOUNT STUDENT, 20, HOSPITALIZED.

No one in Heath Cottage talked of anything else for days. The atmosphere of hysteria prevailed but it was a strained and controlled sort of hysteria. We sought one another's company like shipwreck survivors. I hadn't been a witness to the smoke, the fire, the alarms, the screams, but Cassie would tell and retell the story so vividly it quickly came to seem that, yes, I'd been there, in my room. I'd seen Drew's bleeding hands and I'd seen my friend Marisa carried out of the house strapped to a stretcher, raving, semi-conscious, bright blood smeared on her face and hair.

I would imagine I'd seen Marisa's slashed

99

arms but probably, no, the emergency medical workers had quickly tourniqueted her arms and swathed them in bandages.

'Wait. What did you hear first? Did you hear the alarm, or did you hear Drew?'

I had to know, I plied Cassie with questions. Her account of what had happened differed in some minor details from Dominique's account, and Penelope's. The campus paper reported a chronology of events as Catamount township police determined them, and campus security confirmed, so there came to be a consensus of *what had happened* in the early hours of that Saturday morning. Yet somehow it didn't seem complete, there must have been something missing.

What I knew was: sometime around one A.M. of December 5, Marisa went downstairs into the laundry room of the residence and barricaded the door, which didn't lock, with a stack of vinyl chairs and a heavy wooden bench; she wadded towels around the edge of the door; she dribbled lighter fluid on pages torn from her journal and on miscellaneous items of clothing that happened to be drying in the room; she set a fire, which blazed up swiftly; she'd brought with her a razor blade with which she slashed at her forearms, unable to strike very deeply; she'd taken a triple dose of her prescription Valium; she was wearing one of her Indian muslin floral skirts with a soiled T-shirt; she was barefoot. Drew Weldon,

100

a senior, captain of the rowing team, had passed Marisa on the first-floor stairs carrying a lumpy laundry bag—She was staring through me like a zombie, I knew something was seriously wrong. That poor kid was starving herself to death, too.' After a few minutes Drew followed Marisa down into the basement, and discovered the door barricaded, and smelled the lighter fluid, and the smoke; she tried to open the door, and pounded on it; she was shouting for help, as the smoke detector alarms went off; she managed to force the door open a few inches, and tried to squeeze inside, and there was Marisa, coughing and choking from the smoke but 'just wild, crazy-wild and strong like a wildcat,' slashing at Drew with a razor blade. So Drew fled. She ran upstairs crying for help. By this time the fire alarm was on full blast in the residence and Catamount firemen had been summoned and would arrive within minutes.

'To save Marisa's life.'

Cassie said, 'Yes. I guess. What's left of Marisa's life.'

*   *   *

But I hadn't been a witness to any of this. At the time of Marisa's breakdown I'd been with Dorcas and Andre Harrow in the house on Brierly Lane.

16. *The Intern*

DECEMBER 1975

The distinction between 'assistant' and 'intern' is a simple one: assistants are paid, interns are not.

But of course interns are paid, in experience.

*   *   *

Through December 1975 and into mid-January 1976 I was Dorcas's intern. My internship was 'official'—if anyone from Catamount College should inquire. My duties varied. There were no 'set hours.' Sometimes they neglected to call me for days. And sometimes . . .

It was a secret, this connection. I understood that there were other Catamount girls, and other girls and women in the area, who were, from time to time, involved with Dorcas and Andre Harrow, and there was to be no communication between us. Dorcas and Andre warned me: *Tell no one!* Yet there were those in Heath Cottage who seemed to know, or to guess, and who whispered enviously among themselves.

I saw their eyes. Their eyes moving on me.

Even Cassie, my friend. I saw the questioning in her eyes and turned from her. I was sick with anxiety that I might be found out (but I was twenty years old, hardly a child) but I was suffused with pride, too. *Now I'm blessed. I'm not like anyone else. They love me.*

Though Dorcas warned me not to speak of love.

'You know better, *chérie*, eh? You, so superior to those silly little girls. It only offends him.'

Dorcas, too, framed my face in her hands. Where I'd believed myself ugly, Dorcas saw beauty. Her strong thumbs tugged at the soft skin beside my eyes. She refused to let me speak of my mother—who, at that time, was calling me often, begging me to come home for a weekend; she told me, '*Chérie,* don't be *tîdieuce.*'

To Dorcas and Andre Harrow, the cardinal sin was to be boring.

All else is allowed us, if we are not boring.

I loved it when Dorcas called me *chérie*, like a glamorous Frenchwoman in a movie. No one had ever called me *chérie* before. Dorcas kissed me on the lips, a kiss that stung like fire.

*   *   *

The house at 99 Brierly Lane. How happy I was there! It wasn't the wine—or the *médecine*—that made me euphoric. It was the

104

knowledge that never again would Gillian have to crouch outside in the dripping woods like a beast.

I was tempted to tell Dorcas and Andre. Several times, in a weakened state. How I'd once spied on them. How I'd seen a girl with them one night . . . Marisa? Or no, probably not Marisa. It wouldn't have been prudent for me to mention Marisa's name, under the circumstances.

(Marisa was departed forever from Catamount. We had news of her hospitalization in a Manhattan clinic. Since her breakdown, there'd been no more fires or fire alarms on campus.)

That first night, when Andre Harrow brought me to Dorcas, the house had seemed enormous, behind snow-laden trees. Overhead there was a faint, fading moon. Boldly Andre opened a side door, pushed me inside and called, 'Dorcas! *Une petite surprise.*'

His fascination with Dorcas was absolute. Her fascination with him. No one could ever come between. I'd known that, I think. It was the one clear fact I would know.

The interior of the old New England house was lush as a jungle. Two cultures had collided and the weaker, the New England, had succumbed. Everywhere were Dorcas's things: orchids in earthenware pots, garishly colored woven rugs and wall hangings, Spanish and Mexican tiles. And Dorcas's unframed canvases and carvings that spilled over from the studio into all the rooms. The kitchen was old-fashioned and not very clean—a patina of grime lay over the counters, stove, floor. One day, on my hands and knees, this intern would scrub the stained, sticky linoleum floor. Residing in the kitchen was an aged South American parrot with vivid green and crimson feathers—'Xipe Totec,' Dorcas called him. An Aztec deity? Dorcas's speech was so accented, often I couldn't understand her. She'd been living in the United States for nearly fifteen years, yet made no effort to speak English clearly. This was Dorcas's style. She spoke of Xipe Totec as a 'reincarnated soul,' a 'wicked soul,' the 'god of sacrifice.' He had many times died, she said, 'Yet always, out of his own blood, is reborn.'

Xipe Totec was a fierce, bedraggled creature. One of his beady eyes looked loose in its socket. His sharp curved beak had a hairline crack. His breast feathers were thin and speckled with blood, for he pecked at himself, out of 'deviltry,' as Dorcas said.

Andre said, pouring wine for the three of us, with a gesture at the parrot, 'It's nearing the hour of Xipe Totec's next death. That's why he misbehaves.'

Andre and Dorcas clicked their wineglasses against mine. I saw that my glass was clouded, not very clean; but I drank. The wine was dark, warm, rich, delicious. Dorcas laughed in delight; I'd spilled wine on myself like an eager, clumsy child.

They took turns kissing me. Licking my bruised, sticky mouth.

'Voilà, une petite surprise! Un morceau delicieux.'

'Une belle little animal, eh?'

In Dorcas's studio the carved-wood figures looked alive. I gazed at them in wonder, and dread. How strange that faces and bodies so crudely stylized, so humanly deformed, should take on the quickness of life. Dorcas's genius. It must be in the eyes, I thought. I feared those eyes . . . I knew they would bore into my soul; I would shrink from them through my life.

Yet the eyes were nothing more than holes crudely fashioned in wood.

Our primitive ancestors. Dorcas called them 'totems.' They were tall, hulking; the smallest was six feet, except for an infant head in the shape of a distended sphere, about three feet in diameter. The nursing mother with grotesquely swollen breasts. The gaunt—dying?—nursing mother. The bony, coy adolescent girl who was my sister-self. The plump, preening, adolescent girl cupping her breasts in both hands. The pregnant woman with the belly that swelled like a malignant growth. The squatting woman-giving-birth, an ugly infant's head peeping from her wounded vagina. The skeletal man with an anguished 'O' for a mouth. The muscled man with enormous erect genitals. The fat, old man with empty staring eyes and idiot mouth. The gaunt old ones, their sexual organs withered, with death's-head grins. And the infant head ... On a worktable were a number of infant heads of various sizes, most of them lacking even rudimentary bodies. Dorcas fitted these to 'maternal figures': no bodies, just heads. The effect was sinister. The first night, I hid my eyes and began shivering uncontrollably. Dorcas and Andre Harrow laughed. Andre stroked my hair and the sensitive nape of my neck. Dorcas was sketching us. Her strong, bare arms moved swiftly. Later, she would take Polaroids. Andre would take Polaroids. Our lovemaking was confused and fantastical as a film run faster and faster until it burst into flame.

*   *   *

A night in December.

It may have been several nights ...

I was to help Dorcas pack and crate one of her totems for shipping to a buyer in Palm Springs, California. I was to help Dorcas prepare supper. But I kept falling asleep, I was such a silly little *poupée* ... Xipe Totec, the brightly feathered parrot, shrieked at us. He disliked me in the kitchen. He was jealous of Dorcas's attention. He'd nipped the back of my hand, and made a feint at my eye. Yet

Dorcas and Andre allowed him out of his cage, careening about loose in the kitchen from perch to perch and leaving large, oozing droppings on the floor, on the plank table at which we ate, even on the counter where I was to chop onions but kept almost cutting off the tips of my fingers. (It was my duty to clean up after Xipe Totec, with wetted paper towels.) Rock music played loudly, a European band of whom I'd never heard, a coarser version of the Rolling Stones. Andre was in a dangerous mood. Still, Dorcas laughed at him. *Un pénis maussade.* I'd been absent from my classes for much of the week, including Mr. Harrow's poetry workshop. This was funny! Dorcas called the office of the dean of students to explain that her intern had succumbed to flu—'She has gone home early, and will be back in January.' (In fact I would not be going home to Westchester County. My home was 99 Brierly Lane.) At midnight we sat down to eat, at last. Now Janis Joplin was singing. Xipe Totec was furious with Joplin and outshrieked her. He dared to nip at Andre's knuckles, and had to be forcibly returned to his grime-encrusted cage with the little door locked and the cage hooded with its dark canvas cover, which had the perverse power to put him to sleep. 'What a perfect little male beast he is, with feathers!' Dorcas laughed gaily.

Dorcas had prepared a rich heavy cassoulet. It was delicious though the rice was gummy.

We drank rich, red Italian wine. I lifted my fork to my mouth but it was heavy as lead . . . Both Dorcas and Andre smoked intermittently through the meal: Dorcas, her favorite American filter tips; Andre, the elegant, brown Dutch cigarillos that smelled like burning corncobs. Both urged their choices on me and laughed when I coughed and choked. But their laughter was affectionate. I basked in that laughter like a dog that has been kicked but is now being petted, and is grateful.

They loved me, I think. If desire is love. Not always but sometimes. That night, certainly.

The times were confused. As in a film in which scenes are dreamily spliced together. For I saw often the glisten of blood on Andre's wanly erect penis. I saw the glisten of blood on his coarse pubic hair, and the white, flaccid skin of his abdomen. The warm penumbra of light made by the crook-necked lamp on his desk. Though after that first time, we were never together in his office. *An exquisite little doll you are. So little. I don't want to hurt the doll. I don't want to hurt the doll . . .* A cry of shocked surprise leapt from him, his face crumpled as if he'd been shot.

*   *   *

'For Christ's sake, wake her.'

'*You* wake her. You caused this.'

One of them pressed a hand against my

110

burning forehead. One of them touched an artery below my jaw. 'She's alive, don't be ridiculous.'

'She isn't breathing . . .'

'Yes, she is breathing!'

'I told you no, no fucking Quaaludes. You always have to have your way.'

'Get some ice, I know what to do.'

'Get it yourself! This is your fault.'

Amid the sweaty, rumpled bedclothes I was floating. And suddenly there was a cruel burning sensation against my face, my breasts, and belly . . . So icy-cold it was fire. My eyes flew open, the lashes stuck together. I was awake but couldn't see clearly. My eyelids blinked, fearing flashbulbs.

Not Dorcas's studio but upstairs in the room with the waterstained, peeling wallpaper. Where scented candles blazed. The bed was high, old-fashioned—a New England four-poster. It had a hard mattress, there was something lumpy beneath my hips. When I'd been examined by our doctor in Westchester, to complete my college application, I'd stiffened, cringed, began to cry when the speculum was inserted. It was punishment I knew: for being a girl. The doctor had expressed impatience. My mother (in the waiting room) had told me nervously it had to be done, it was . . . a procedure. Not the procedure but the girl is to blame. The figures looming over me now were gigantic as

111

those looming over an infant's crib. I began to whimper, and one of them quickly pressed a hand over my mouth.

That shrieking parrot! I'd thought it was Xipe Totec but (evidently) it was the girl.

17. *Guilt*

DECEMBER 1975

We were in the first-floor lounge at Heath Cottage talking in lowered voices about Marisa.

Marisa who was gone. Marisa who was 'hospitalized.'

As if the enemy were just outside the door, Dominique said sullenly, 'Let the bastards prove Marisa did those fires! Or anything else, y'know? The false alarms.'

Penelope said, 'How could they prove any of it? If they couldn't prove it at the time? Nobody was thinking of Marisa then. And there aren't any fingerprints or anything.'

Cassie said bitterly, 'They said she "confessed." That was just to hurt herself more. I know that feeling!'

Dominique said, incensed, 'Well, she's changed her mind now. "Recanted."'

I listened to my friends' voices like music around me. I was in a state of nervous suspension. It seemed to me that, like a clever child, I'd performed an unexpected feat. Yet no one of my friends knew.

She isn't breathing.

Yes, she's breathing!

I heard myself saying, 'It's hard to expunge

something like that from your record, though. If you confess. Like pleading guilty in court. Her lawyer can argue she was in mental anguish, I guess . . .'

Dominique turned furiously to me. '*You* think Marisa did it?'

I was stunned by Dominique's response. I wiped at my eyes. I said, stammering, 'Everybody w-wants to think so.'

'Sure! But *you*?'

I shook my head. No.

(But maybe Marisa had? If not all the fires, then several? One or two? And the false alarms? How could any of us know?)

My friends' eyes bored through me. They distrusted me. I knew how they thought of me: their jealousy. Their surprise. Their resentment. Yet they had to be admiring, didn't they? If they guessed. (Did they guess?) I had told no one of my friends that I was Dorcas's intern and that they would be taking me with them to Paris later that month. *Chérie, you have never been? What a pity.*

Dominique's sharp, black eyes snagging onto me, pondering . . .

Cassie was saying, 'It's ridiculous: how could Marisa prove she's innocent, now? Like, even if she'd been away from Catamount at the time of some of the fires, with her boyfriend in New York, for instance, they could twist it around and say she came back to campus undetected. If they want to pin all this crap on her.'

114

Penelope said worriedly, 'Still. There haven't been any fires, since. Or false alarms.'

We laughed uneasily. We joked that we should set a small fire, soon. At least pull an alarm. 'To help out Marisa, right?'

Penelope, who was the most dogged of us, said, 'What everybody says, though—how likely is it, there'd be two arsonists? A place this small?'

Dominique said impatiently, 'Arson is copycat stuff. You read the papers.'

Cassie said, 'Maybe it's an adult? One of the faculty? Nobody ever suggests that. Why's it so weird?'

We considered this. It wasn't very persuasive.

'People want it to be Marisa,' I said. 'She came along at the right time.'

'Which doesn't make the arsonist Marisa, does it?'

In the doorway there hovered a husky girl named Joan, a senior, a friend of Drew Weldon. She hoped to join us to offer her opinion but we'd been freezing her out. Now I glanced up at her with a smile, as if I'd only just become aware of her, and she took this as an invitation to come into the lounge.

Joan said, wide-eyed with sympathy, 'Poor Marisa! But if she did it, y'know . . . she needs help, bad.'

Dominique said rudely, 'She didn't. That's bullshit.'

115

Joan looked at us, confused. 'Marisa didn't
. . . set the fire? Downstairs?'

Dominique said, '*That* fire. Who's talking
about that pissy little fire? We're talking about
the others.'

'But she confessed, didn't she?'

Penelope said, ignoring Joan, 'But how can
Marisa prove she's innocent, now? See, once
she confessed. Even if it was a false confession.
It's in the papers and in her record. Even with
this lawyer—'

Joan interrupted, 'Will there be a trial?'

Cassie said stiffly, 'I don't think so. Marisa is
. . . what they say "unfit to stand trial." She's
pretty sick.'

'I guess. That's so sad. She used to be so
pretty, didn't she? So much energy. Drew said,
down in the laundry room, she was, well . . .
"deranged." Totally.'

'She'd been starving herself. She was
anorexic.'

'I'd try to get her to eat,' Cassie said, 'and
when she did, it was like her stomach was
bloated, I guess; she couldn't wait to escape
from me and get to a bathroom . . .'

We thought of Marisa. The last time
I'd seen her was in Mr. Harrow's poetry
workshop. So exhilarated, basking in our
attention, you could see a blue vein quivering
in her forehead and you could feel the heat
from her skin across the table. Her hair hadn't
been washed or combed in days and her eyes

116

looked like glazed blue marbles . . . Andre Harrow had stared at her, considering.

But Dorcas had favored Gillian at that time.

Joan said, 'Are any of you in contact with Marisa? Or her family?'

Cassie and Penelope murmured yes, sort of. But this wasn't exactly true. Dominique shoved out her fleshy, lower lip and said nothing. It was then that she glanced at me, saw me looking at her, and winked.

Not a friendly wink, though.

*   *   *

Afterward we'd realize, we never spoke of Sybil any longer.

18. The Tease

'Jill-y! Ain't you gonna wait an' walk with yo' Dommie?'

Like warm, brown molasses there came Dominique's voice calling after me as I walked hurriedly along the icy path to the chapel.

This was a sly, cruel tease. The mock-Negroid accent. And—*Dommie*! As if my arrogant friend would have allowed such an infantile diminution of her elegant name.

I waited for Dominique to catch up. In our relationship she was the more powerful and seductive, as she was the more resentful.

Beautiful Dominique. Now she wore her scintillant, black hair in cornrows that swung about her head with an air both of jubilance and menace.

We walked together in the bright, cold air. I was feeling shy of Dominique, yet hopeful. Of the girls in Heath, it was Dominique I most admired. Now that she'd revealed her 'Barbadoan brown background,' she seemed yet more elusive. I wondered if Andre Harrow had been as surprised as the rest of us in the workshop and had to think, yes, he was.

Since that afternoon Dominique seemed to be avoiding her Heath Cottage friends. She

119

rarely ate meals with us now, but with other black girls in the dining hall: theirs was a noisy, festive table which Caucasians regarded uneasily. Some of the girls at this table were American blacks, wearing their hair Afro-style or in cornrows, but others were from the Caribbean and spoke English with crisp Brit accents. Caucasians courted them shyly, but with limited success. Now Dominique publicly aligned herself with them. She represented a coup for them—gorgeous Dominique Landau, who was a dancer, a poet, a campus personality. When I saw her with her new friends I felt a pang of loss. In their company, Dominique did look like one of them. Her olive-dark, flawless complexion, dazzling, white smile and long-lashed, black eyes . . .

In our residence, Dominique was curt and abrupt with me. If I said hello, she might respond with a drawling, 'Uhhuh,' meant as a verbal ditto. In Andre Harrow's workshop she rarely had a word of praise for anything I wrote; she stared at me, and at Mr. Harrow, plumping out her lower lip sullenly. I thought, *She knows.*

One of Dorcas's sturdy, voluptuous female totems, with high, pertly rounded buttocks and beautifully shaped breasts, hips, and thighs, and a strong-jawed face, I believed might be modeled upon Dominique.

She knows. But she can't be certain.

At the chapel, Dominique paused as if

120

reluctant to let me go. Our long holiday break began the following Monday. I'd asked Dominique where she was going, and she shrugged indifferently: 'Same old Aspen-skiin'. My daddy's got these chummy honkies he sucks up to, y'know?'

I felt the sting of that word—*honkey.* I wondered if it was the equivalent of *nigger.*

'You're going home, are you? Where's it— Westchester?'

I murmured yes. This was what I'd been telling my friends.

Dominique peered at me, smiling. That sly, slow suggestive smile.

Impulsively I said, 'The other day, I realized—we don't talk about Sybil any longer. It's like she has ceased to exist.'

'Sybil *who*?'

I laughed, startled.

'Hell, girl. I guess that ain't funny.'

I hated Dominique's mock-Negroid manner. Yet I supposed I could understand its origin.

Before we moved on, Dominique caught sight of my hand; the back of my right hand, which was covered in scratches and small scabs. She took hold of my hand and squeezed it hard and said, incensed, 'Who's been peckin' you, honey? Some nasty ol' green parrot? I'd put a stop to *that.*'

I drew my hand away. I turned and entered the chapel without a backward glance.

19. *Soul Murder*

DECEMBER 1975

'Gillian, do you believe in evil?'

Penelope spoke quietly. Almost, I might have pretended I hadn't heard.

It was four P.M. of Friday, December 16. The campus was emptying out. After a flurry of activity, Heath Cottage was nearly deserted. In the downstairs lounge Penelope and I stood at the window, waiting for her parents to arrive from Old Saybrook, Connecticut, to drive her home for the holidays. We were watching a languid snowfall.

The pretense was that, early next morning, I was taking a train to New York. To my mother.

'Evil? No.' I spoke quickly, embarrassed.

'Just "no"?'

'Not in the old way. I don't think so.'

'What's the "old way"?'

I wasn't sure. But I needed to speak. Andre Harrow would have been furious with me if I'd kept silent.

I said, 'God and Satan. "Good" and "evil." A supernatural principle.'

'There's no evil, without the supernatural?' Penelope crinkled her forehead. Her fair, moon-shaped face was comically incongruous with her theological concern.

I recalled that Penelope, in our Intro to Philosophy class, freshman year, never grasped the fundamental fact that logic has nothing to do with truth, only with premises. I'd tutored her, but her final grade was C+.

I said, 'In the Bible, Satan is the father of lies, and of all evil. In our world, "evil" just seems to be something people do out of their own self-interest, and others object. What's "good" is what our side does.'

Penelope said sharply, 'It's that simple?'

You hate me. You're jealous. He doesn't love you.

I was staring out the window. A dreamy, hypnotic snowfall, no wind. Outside the residence the hill loomed steep and snowy. There were shoveled paths to the quadrangle, and beyond toward the tennis courts and the playing fields and Catamount Creek and the woods . . .

'There's such a thing as soul murder,' Penelope said. 'Except you can't see it, the way you see the other. There are evil people. Cruel people. People who should be punished. If there was anyone to punish them.'

I would be joining Dorcas and Andre in a few hours. My heartbeat quickened in anticipation, and apprehension.

When Penelope's parents arrived I walked outside with her, helping to carry her things. Her mother leaned out of the car, smiling happily. 'Sybil! How are you, dear?'

124

Penelope said stiffly, 'This is Gillian, Mom. You've met Gillian.'

'Oh, of course. Gillian.'

I waved at them as they drove away. A sudden turn, in the slow-falling snow, and they were gone.

20. Winter Break

It had been a misunderstanding, obviously.

I'd thought from what they were saying that they would take me with them. To Paris. Had I misheard? But I smiled quickly now to show that I understood.

'Just fifteen days, *chérie*,' Dorcas said, squeezing my hand, 'then we will celebrate the New Year, yes? Just us.'

They were scheduled to leave sooner than I'd seemed to know. I helped Dorcas with her packing, while Andre was on the phone much of the afternoon. I overheard him cursing. Yet he laughed, too. Evidently there had been other misunderstandings.

'We'll reschedule. Next month. Good-bye!'

When Andre saw my face, the hurt and shock in my face, he frowned irritably and looked away. That flicker of guilt. So that I knew in that instant, *He wants to take me, but not her. He loves me.* There was some confusion about the dates, the plane tickets, the times of departure and of arrival.

I wondered if another intern would be meeting them at Kennedy. Another girl, a Catamount girl, perhaps one of my predecessors, who'd purchased her own tickets, as I couldn't have done.

I would be in charge of the house, however. It was my responsibility to water the plants, bring in and sort the mail, feed Xipe Totec. The upstairs rooms would be shut off, unheated. I was not to go upstairs. Dorcas's studio also would be shut. But the kitchen and the living room would be heated. 'We're depending upon you, Gillian. Will you miss us?'

When it was time to say good-bye Andre framed my face in his hands and kissed my forehead lightly. Still he was avoiding my eyes; I wished he'd look at me so that I could forgive him. Dorcas was more passionate, wrapping me in her strong arms, kissing my mouth. Afterward I would discover a smear of crimson on my chin. Dorcas had made up her face white as a geisha's and her eyes were enlarged with mascara and blue eyeshadow like neon. In my ear she whispered loudly, 'I will make it up to you, *chérie*. I promise.'

*   *   *

So my winter break was spent in solitude, mostly.

I missed them terribly. But when I was in their house I could pretend they were in the next room, or upstairs. When I entered Dorcas's studio I could pretend that Dorcas was working just out of my line of vision. I

128

walked among the hulking totems, gazing up at them in wonder. Always it seemed strange to me, uncanny, that such primitive figures, hardly more than hunks of untreated wood with rudimentary human features, and blank eyes, should seem more alive than I.

Dutifully I brought in the mail and sorted it. I kept the front walk shoveled. I watered the plants, I fed the parrot, and cleaned up after him. If the phone rang while I was in the house I answered it, identifying myself as Dorcas's intern, Gillian; I recorded messages carefully. There were galleries in Tucson, Seattle, Palm Springs, Toronto where Dorcas placed her totems; her sales were sporadic, but continuous. I knew from remarks I'd overheard between Dorcas and Andre that she scorned New York City; maybe she'd had a bad experience there.

I'd gathered, too, that Andre Harrow had written poetry, once.

He'd composed music, too. In the mid-sixties. A long time ago, as he said. 'All gone up in flame.'

*   *   *

The big untidy kitchen was Xipe Totec's domain. When I entered, the green-feathered parrot shrieked angrily. 'Al-*lo*! Al-*lo*! Al-*lo*!'

In my naiveté I'd thought that Xipe Totec would become my friend. He was a lonely

129

creature, now that his mistress and master were gone. He pecked at his breast, tore out feathers and drew blood in a fury of frustration, but he preferred his loneliness to my companionship. Though I fed him, kept his water dish fresh, cleaned up after him. Though I talked to him, even sang to him. His mad, loose eye fixed upon me malevolently and his scaly claws twitched, but he didn't fly at me to attack. A parrot is the most intelligent of birds: this one might have gauged the differences in our sizes and he might have reasoned that, if I grabbed him in self-defense, I could overpower him.

Dorcas remarked that Xipe Totec was an aging bird, which accounted for his *méchant* behavior. Once he'd been young, filled with energy, delightful. He'd perched on her shoulder, cooed and nuzzled in her ear. He'd called her *chérie* and he'd been her *chérie*.

I pressed my hands over my ears, entering the kitchen where Xipe Totec awaited me, trembling in his cage. 'Al-*lo*! Al-*lo*!' he screeched, as if warding off an evil spirit.

*   *   *

I had not been forbidden to go upstairs, exactly. It was not in the spirit of Dorcas and Andre Harrow to 'forbid.' But of course I ventured upstairs, after a few days. I told myself I was lonely for them. I wanted to be

130

closer to them.

By day the bedroom was almost an ordinary room. The wallpaper was stained near the ceiling and beginning to peel. There was too much furniture for the space. But it was sumptuously decorated: the four-poster bed was covered with a richly embroidered Mexican quilt; there were wall hangings, plush chairs. A bureau with an enormous mirror. I opened the bureau drawers to examine the clothing inside, Dorcas's silky, satiny things, Andre's more pragmatic white cotton underwear. I opened the door to a drafty walk-in closet and inhaled the stale perfumy tobacco-y smell.

They'd known I would come up here, I thought. They had willed it.

She isn't breathing . . .

She is!

Adjacent to the bedroom was a study of Andre's. Here he had a desk, a filing cabinet, sagging bookshelves crammed with books, most of them paperbacks. On one wall was a Grateful Dead poster from the psychedelic sixties. How remote it seemed, though I'd been living then. There was a foot-high wooden carving of Dorcas's on a windowsill: the thick-muscled man with the semi-erect penis. His head was small for his body, his face brute and nearly blank.

I am my penis, I am purely animal. I endure.

I sat at Andre's desk, in his swivel chair. I

131

wrote rapidly in my journal, scattered thoughts I would later discard. I stared at the shelves of books that oppressed me, there were so many. What were the secrets contained here? Would I ever understand them? *The Complete Poems of D. H. Lawrence. The Feathered Serpent. Apocalypse. Lady Chatterley's Lover. Aaron's Rod. Kangaroo. The Woman Who Rode Away. Sons and Lovers. The Escaped Cock. The Lost Girl.*

The filing cabinet, which consisted of three deep drawers, was locked. But eventually I found the key, taped to the underside of the desk.

In these drawers were financial records, insurance documents, files of poems in fading carbon copies. A slender, cheaply printed chapbook titled, *Icarus Poems,* by Andre Harrow, City Lights Press, 1967. (The poems seemed to have been influenced by e. e. cummings and Allen Ginsberg. I became distracted reading them, and stopped.) And there were loose, bulging files held together by rubber bands: photographs, hand-drawn sketches of Dorcas's, and magazines.

I took these out. I felt as if someone had struck me a numbing blow between the shoulder blades.

In the first file, on top, were a dozen Polaroid shots of a giddy, disheveled girl with long messy hair who resembled me.

In these photos and rapidly drawn sketches

132

the girl was dressed, part-dressed, and at last naked. Initially she was lying on the downstairs living room sofa, a plush, thickly cushioned piece of furniture made of crimson velvet; next, she was posed on a floor, glassy-eyed, smiling idiotically, her small breasts drooping obscenely thin, like bananas. She was covered in perspiration and her bruised-looking mouth glistened with saliva. Semen?

Most of the poses were of the girl by herself, like an anatomical specimen. But in several photos a man and a woman appeared, separately: a naked man crouching over her as she lay naked and spread-eagled on a bed, the man seen only from the back; a stout, fleshy woman, also seen from the back, clothed, with dyed-red hair spilling luxuriously over her shoulders.

What were they doing to the silly, semi-conscious girl . . . ?

Here is evidence. Chérie is loved!

In other files were dozens, maybe hundreds of photos and sketches of girls. They must have dated back for a decade. And porn magazines with names like *X-Rated, SEX Confidential, Adults Only.* Several of these magazines were opened to pages where photographs had been reprinted. In the pulp magazines, the girls' faces were cut out or censored by black rectangles. Adults were faceless, seen only from the rear.

My hands shook, lifting these. Would my

photo turn up in a porn magazine; had that been their intention all along . . . ?

Chérie, how beautiful you are! Look at our chérie.

I stared at graphic sex scenes. Cartoonlike, ugly. Some were posed, the girls leering drunkenly into the camera lens; others were candid shots, blurred. The girls were young and attractive and dazed. Some were lying semi-conscious, their slender limbs arranged in revealing positions, like cadavers about to be dissected. Suddenly I saw a girl I thought I recognized: she'd been a senior at Catamount when I was a freshman. A flamboyant drama major, with a reputation for promiscuity and drugs. She was naked, kneeling in front of a man with dark, peltlike chest hair, a stocky body, obviously not Andre Harrow; her mouth was open, shaped in a foolish grin. Subsequent Polaroids showed a sex act at which I couldn't bring myself to look, which was reproduced in a two-page spread in *X-Rated*, October 1973. And there—was it Penelope? Penelope! Or a girl with a round, childlike face who closely resembled Penelope—seated on the downstairs sofa, naked from the waist up, solemnly cupping her breasts as if offering them to the viewer. In a related sketch, the girl lay on her back sprawled and simpering like a lewd doll.

I wanted to snatch up and tear into pieces this evidence of my friend's degradation. Yet

134

for some reason I could not, as I'd been unable to destroy evidence of my own.

Among a cache of strangers there was sulky Dominique: beautiful in her nakedness, voluptuous in an odalisque pose, one knee raised and her hooded eyes shut as if unconscious of, or indifferent to, the camera. In other subsequent shots, Dominique—or this velvety light-skinned black girl who so resembled Dominique—was joined by a man, and by a woman, seen exclusively from the back. And there was Marisa: no mistaking Marisa, in the odalisque pose, against the same crimson background, the downstairs sofa; her pretty, delicate face looking brittle as a doll's, as if it might easily break. There were as many as twenty shots and sketches of Marisa, made at different times. In the most disturbing, Marisa lay naked and a man with a blemished back and raddled waist stooped over her, spreading her legs, fingers sunk into the slender flesh of her inner thighs. The photo exposed Marisa's face in painful detail, but the man was anonymous, protected. In another series of photos, apparently taken upon another occasion, Marisa was posed with Sybil, arms around each other's waist, standing before one of Dorcas's female totems; in some of the shots they wore clingy, flimsy, Indian-muslin costumes through which you could see their shadowy groins and breasts, in other shots the girls were naked. They cavorted together, clowning for the camera like demented children.

In the ugliest shot, which was also a pastel sketch, Sybil was naked on her knees as someone, his figure blurred in the foreground, was lifting her by a leather belt looped around her neck. Sybil's expression was strained, ecstatic. *See how I submit to you. See how I adore you.* The older photographs were of strangers. And the photographs in the porn magazines. Girls I didn't recognize. Some looked like locals, girls and women with heavily made-up faces and teased hair. In one, a girl who looked no older than thirteen was on all fours, blood running in two nearly symmetrical streams from her small snubbed nose; she wore a lacy, black half-slip and ridiculous high-heeled shoes. In another, the same girl was seated in a straight-backed cane chair, a chair I recognized from the kitchen, one in which, in fact, I'd sat on for meals, smiling dreamily at the camera while behind her stood a stout-bodied woman, head cut off by the camera, lifting her long, wavy, fair-brown hair in two thick strands above her shoulders, like a trophy. There were men, too; young men mostly, seen partially or from the back. A few were teenagers. One, I thought I recognized: the man who'd called after Dorcas outside the post office . . .

I thought, *They want me to find these. They're*

136

proud of these.

I wondered if they assumed I'd be proud, too.

There was a dull roaring in my ears. A sensation of numbness. I felt sick, sickened. But I did nothing except return the photos, sketches, magazines to the filing cabinet as if they'd never been disturbed.

I returned the key, taped, to the underside of the desk.

I went downstairs. Still I was numbed, unreal. If a plan was taking shape in my mind, as a dream begins to form itself, by day, out of the residue of the day, to burst into splendor by night, I had no awareness of it. I was wakened from my trance by a maniacal shrieking—'Al-*lo*! Al-*lo*!' Instinctively I crouched, and shielded my face, as the flailing wings rushed overhead.

* * *

Two days later was Christmas Eve. I telephoned my mother to forestall her trying to call me.

137

21. The New Year

They'd been drugged. Like me.
They'd been in love. Like me.
They would keep these secrets forever. Like me.
We are beasts and this is our consolation.

*   *   *

'Gillian, my God. What's happened to you?'

It was the New Year, and a new semester at Catamount College.

I signed up for new courses. I'd been approved for the continuation of Mr. Harrow's small, elite poetry workshop.

I'd taken incompletes in two fall-semester courses: biology and European history. In a third course, Renaissance literature, I'd received an unexpected grade of B-, even though I'd been absent intermittently for weeks and a few hours after the final exam couldn't remember a thing I'd written. The dean of students believed that Gillian Brauer had been sick with a severe case of flu—'That nasty Asian flu that's going around this winter.' It was plausible, and maybe it was true. I felt a mild nausea much of the time,

139

spreading through my body like fever. One day in the bathroom Cassie suddenly pulled at my flannel nightgown, staring at my waist. 'Gillian, you've gotten so *thin.*'

I snatched the material away from Cassie's fingers. I had nothing to say to our nosey Heath Cottage Cassandra.

*   *   *

They're jealous. They hate me. What do they know, they know nothing.

*   *   *

Dorcas and Andre were back from Europe, I knew. I'd left the house cleaned, the mail sorted in careful piles on the plank table in the kitchen, a conscientious account of phone messages. I'd hiked a mile to the Safeway in the village, to purchase some of Dorcas's and Andre's favorite breakfast foods; I knew they would be arriving in Catamount late. I scrubbed Xipe Totec's bamboo cage as clean as I could get it, enduring the bird's outraged squawks and beak-feints at my hands. As Dorcas had instructed, I left the key to the house beneath the front doormat.

And I'd shoveled the front walk.

I waited for a call, but no call came. There was no pink slip in my mailbox. I had obsessively rehearsed how I would speak with

140

Dorcas and Andre, how I would betray none of what I knew, but as the days passed I came to doubt whether I knew anything significant, or whether I'd imagined, dreamt . . . whatever it was I'd spread out on the desk in Mr. Harrow's study.

I waited anxiously. I stayed away from the residence so that, when I returned, there might be a miraculous pink slip in my mailbox. Otherwise, if I were in my room and having to listen to the phone ring repeatedly, always for others, I couldn't bear it.

I drifted along the bank of the Catamount Creek, which was frozen solid now. That arctic glisten to the Berkshire hills, crusted with snow hard as ice. The snow was much too deep, and the crust too sharp, to encourage me to make my way through the woods to the back of Brierly Lane. And I was probably too weak; I'd have stumbled and fallen. Climbing the stairs to my room left me panting.

I'd seen Andre Harrow walking across the quad with Michelle and a freckle-faced girl with a loud, pealing, happy laugh. Both Michelle and this girl, Diane Kantrell, were drama majors, highly regarded.

Never had I considered this: that Dorcas and Andre wouldn't contact me at all. I was sick with worry: Did they know? That I'd disobeyed, and gone upstairs? That I'd unlocked the filing cabinet and seen—the evidence? Like a knot that wouldn't untie, at which we keep pulling, picking, prying with our nails until our nails break, this possibility haunted me.

Worse: Were they simply indifferent to me, Dorcas's intern, the faithful house-sitter, and too busy after their European trip to get into touch? Intending to call me, even to invite me over, sometime, but in no haste?

I will make it up to you, chérie. I promise.

*   *   *

At last, before the first meeting of Mr. Harrow's poetry workshop, he spoke to me in the hall where I'd been lingering near his office door, and told me, with a genial smile, that he and Dorcas very much appreciated my overseeing the house, and would be calling me soon. 'Dorcas promises to make one of her cassoulets. And Xipe Totec misses you, and says "Al-*lo*." ' So we laughed together easily.

The workshop met in the same, rather small, seminar room, which quickly became clouded with smoke. There were four new girls in the class, of whom three were smokers. It was an intense, somewhat theoretical class meeting, at which Andre Harrow did most of the talking. He'd trimmed his beard and looked ruddy, dapper. In his left earlobe there glinted a small emerald stud, which was new, and which everyone in the workshop admired. Mr. Harrow inquired genially after

142

our holidays, our winter breaks. Celebrating Christmas, Hannukah. 'These are seasonal, celestial rituals, rooted in our genes. Our animal, atavistic souls. We must celebrate the winter solstice and almost anything will do for us, any dark, sacrificial religion.' We leaned forward, listening intently. Especially the new girls, rapt with the privilege of being in such proximity to Andre Harrow.

*   *   *

Before the next poetry workshop, I cut my hair.

I cut my hair ruthlessly, savagely, ecstatically.

Yet with a purpose: I scissored close to my head, leaving the bulk of my hair uncut. It was shimmering, glinting, beautiful on the newspapers I'd spread on the bathroom floor. Carefully I divided it into two thick strands, and braided these strands, and next day I went to Mr. Harrow's office to present him with the braids which I'd wrapped in tinsel paper like a gift. Mr. Harrow stared at the braids, and at me, at my shorn, small head, and in that instant I saw a look of wonder in his face. *I've surprised you, haven't I. I'm no silly little girl, am I, to be predicted.*

I'd never seen Andre Harrow so stunned, disconcerted. He nearly stammered. 'Gillian, what—what the hell have you done? Your

143

beautiful hair—'

I said proudly, 'Dorcas said she liked it. It was my best feature, Dorcas has always said.'

Mr. Harrow said, 'But should Dorcas always get what she wants?'

I laughed, for this was meant to be a joke.

Mr. Harrow said, now quickly, 'Nobody asked you to do this, Gillian. Yes?'

'Nobody.'

Mr. Harrow lifted one of the braids, stroking it as if it were a live thing. He pressed it against his cheek, sniffed its fragrance, in a way that made me weak with desire. Then he rewrapped it in the tinsel. He said, 'Dorcas will want to see you, I'm sure. She'll call tonight.'

We'd been speaking quietly. In case another girl was in the hall outside the door, hoping to overhear.

*   *   *

(Had Dorcas and Andre discovered I'd opened the filing cabinet? It didn't seem so at that time. Nor would I ever know.)

22. The Fire

19 JANUARY 1976

And so, yes. Dorcas did call me. And so I returned to the house in the cul-de-sac of Brierly Lane.

The old New England farmhouse nearly hidden by juniper pines, birches. Where snow-laden evergreens sagged with that look of winter stoicism. That indomitable will that is the will of all life to survive.

Dorcas greeted me lavishly. I saw in her eyes that I'd surprised her and that she'd liked the surprise. My small, shorn head—'*Ma petite, what have you done?*'—she gripped in her strong hands, framing, considering. '*Chérie,* you are too cruel to yourself. Now you look, what's your word, eh—*un martyr—comme Jeanne d'Arc.*' Dorcas grabbed me and kissed me wetly and tussled what remained of my hair as you might rub the head of a beloved but foolish dog.

Andre, too, greeted me vigorously. He'd been drinking, like Dorcas; his face was warmly ruddy; in his shrewd eyes was that look I'd seen the previous afternoon in his office.

Nobody asked you to do this. Remember.

Dorcas walked me straight to her studio, to show me how she'd made use of my sacrifice.

145

The braids of the *petite poupée* were prominently displayed on one of the adolescent-girl totems. Not the rail-thin one but the voluptuous one, with shapely breasts, hips, thighs, and a preening stance. Cleverly, Dorcas had attached the braids to the figure's head, which was tilted at a slight angle backward, as if the empty eyes were lifted skyward. Basking in young, burgeoning sexuality. The delusion of young-female power. You believe that, in your beautiful new body, you might live forever.

You believe that, in your beautiful new body, you will be treated with love.

'*Belle,* yes? She has no brain—she is *bête*—but *belle,* yes?'

I laughed, the braids were so convincing on the totem. They were so completely *of the totem*, and no longer mine.

I laughed, wiping at my eyes. There was an awkward moment when the *petite poupée* might have broken down and begun to cry, might have become hysterical, an ugly scene, if, for instance, her face was tear-stricken, her nose running, who would wish to kiss her then? Who would wish to embrace her, undress her, fondle and make use of her compliant body, then?

Fortunately, the moment passed.

*   *   *

Unfortunately, the braids, like the totem, would be lost.

* * *

My memory of the next several hours is confused. My memory of the next forty-eight hours, in fact.

Dorcas insisted upon preparing one of her rich cassoulets. We were hilarious in the kitchen. Dorcas, and Andre, and Gillian. Xipe Totec flailed about shrieking and outraged as if he'd never seen me before, as if I hadn't tended to him for fifteen days—'The bird is jealous of you, *chérie!* He thinks, looking like you do, you are someone he doesn't know, *un étranger méchant.* Foolish bird!'

It was true. The parrot didn't seem to know me any longer. With most of my hair gone, my head looked small, vulnerable as an eggshell. My eyes felt exposed, I shrank from Xipe Totec's flashing beak. Andre cursed the parrot and went to put on gloves, to capture him and return him to his cage. Once the little door was locked, Dorcas slipped the dark hood over the cage. Miraculously, Xipe Totec's squawking ceased at once. In that abrupt darkness he'd be asleep within minutes.

'*Voilà, chérie!* You are safe with us now.'

By the time we sat down to eat I was faint with hunger. The cassoulet was made with sausage and wild duck and I'd never tasted

147

anything so delicious, except after the first several forkfuls my throat shut up tight, I couldn't eat. Dorcas and Andre, unmindful of me, ate voraciously. And drank voraciously. Dorcas's fleshy face shone with the effort of eating, her crimson mouth smeared. She was heavier than I recalled. Andre Harrow, too, had gained weight over the holidays. The skin beneath his eyes was puffy. The minuscule speck of blood in his right eye gleamed like a tiny gem. His and Dorcas's jaws moved like the jaws of giants, grinding. I loved watching them through my fingers. Andre, seeing me, laughed and filled my wineglass another time. My head was empty as an eggshell, the faint, dull headache I'd had for days had vanished. When I tried to lift my glass my hand shook so Andre steadied it. After I drank, Andre kissed my mouth. He said this was Christmas and New Year's Eve combined—'We had to celebrate without you, and we missed you.'

Dorcas cried drunkenly, 'Missed you like hell, *chérie*! And now you have shorn your beautiful hair like a sheep.'

It was then that I did a strange thing: I lay my head on the plank table beside my bowl. I pressed my forehead against the solid wood. I was laughing quietly, I wasn't crying. I whispered, 'It's just that I love you so. I love you both. I'm sorry I've been bad. I can't live without you. I don't want to live without you . . .'

Andre said, lighting up a cigarillo, 'And we don't want you to live without us either, *chérie.*'

*　　*　　*

It was late. The dangerous hour. A telephone rang and Andre lurched to answer it, cursing. Dorcas shouted after him. There was an ongoing quarrel in the air like the smell of scorched food in the heavy cassoulet dish which would be Gillian's task to scour and clean in the morning, if there was a morning. I began to cry with happiness. They walked me between them and over my bent head the quarrel continued. On the stairs my knees buckled, so they carried me. My feet were bare. I was limp, unresisting as a rag doll. It was then that I was sick, suddenly choking and vomiting, which disgusted Dorcas. 'Ugh! *Obscene!*' The hot, smelly liquid spilling from my mouth had splattered onto the bosom of her quilted tunic and onto her shapely small feet in gold-gilt slippers. Dorcas would have let me drop to the floor but Andre held me by the armpits, laughing. Later, Dorcas slapped my face and shoved me out of the room. On hands and knees I crawled. I wasn't certain where I was: at the top of the stairs? The corridor was dark, drafty. I could hear them cursing each other. I understood then, *He wants me, he loves me, but she will keep me from him.* I heard them struggling and grunting together on the high, creaking bed. Their giant jaws had been grinding food and now their bodies would grind each other. I tried to press my hands against my ears but I was too weak. Vomit dribbled down my chin in a long thread. There came a low female groaning. A slow rhythmic thudding that quickened in speed, then slowed; quickened, slowed. A whimpering, rising sound.

They want me to hear, I'm their witness.

By sitting, and sliding myself down step by step, I made my way downstairs. My head was filled with static. My vision was blurred. But I found the rest of my clothing, my jeans and panties, where they'd been plucked from me. I fumbled dressing, my hands shook so badly. Tears were streaming down my hot, hurting face. Then I was panicked I wouldn't find my boots, but finally I found them tossed into the back hall. It took a while to put them on: I had to sit down, and force my feet inside each boot, and when I saw that I'd forced my left foot into the right boot, and my right foot into the left boot, I laughed. I discovered that my fingers were sticky with wine and vomit. I made my way to the sink that was stacked with dirtied plates to wash my hands, and splash cold water onto my face that felt like fever. In his corner beneath his dark canvas hood Xipe Totec slept undisturbed.

As overhead the giants of the household

150

would sleep their sodden, dreamless sleep, sated after sex.

I located my jacket, and my long woolen scarf. It was very cold outside: I would have to walk back to campus in my dazed, weakened state, and my hair gone. My friends would be appalled seeing me; quickly I would flee from them. I knew if our eyes met they would know and they had no business knowing. The confusion in my head was like static that waxed, then waned, then waxed again, deafening. Yet, I would manage to make my way back through the sub-zero dark to Heath Cottage and my room, and my bed. I would not attempt a shortcut through the woods behind the house, I would make my way along Brierly Lane, which was plowed, lined by tall banks of snow. I would make my way to College Road, and to the wrought-iron gates of Catamount College, looming like the gates in an illustrated fairy tale for children. *I will. I will!* All this I would do, exhausted and broken. I would be in my room by three A.M.

Except. I was still in the kitchen, my eyes stinging. The smell! Dorcas would be furious that her intern had crept away, leaving such devastation. The smell of burnt cassoulet was powerful, sickening. In an overflowing ashtray on the plank table was one of Andre's smoldering cigarillos. I went to put it out but instead I carried it into the adjoining living room. There, I placed it on the sofa, on one of

151

the plush, stained crimson cushions. The cigarillo had been smoked to about one-third of its length. A small halo of ash fell off, revealing a gemlike glow. The other end of the cigarillo was damp and chewed. As a child might do, out of curiosity mainly, I rolled the smoldering cigarillo across the cushion. It settled against the back of the cushion and sank just a little, almost out of sight. Was the cigarillo still burning, or had it gone out? I thought probably it had gone out. Yet I smelled its acrid stink. Behind the sofa was an earthenware vase of tall, dried reeds and rushes, sand-colored, beautiful. And flammable.

Against a living room wall was a leaning stack of several of Dorcas's unframed canvases. Her luridly bright Aztec-inspired primitive abstracts. I carried these to lean against the side of the sofa. It was not that I was thinking, *These, too, are flammable.* I was not thinking at all. I moved by instinct.

23. *The Alarm*

20 JANUARY 1976

In the night, sirens erupting.
In the night, the terrible beauty of fire.
A fire alarm in Heath Cottage was pulled at 3:50 A.M. The noise was deafening, heart-stopping. I heard shouts, I heard someone run outside in the hall pounding on our doors—'Fire!' Within seconds we staggered from our beds into the now brightly lit hall and down the front stairs to the nearest exit, which was the front door of the residence. We smelled smoke, faintly. We had no idea how far away the fire was.

I thought, *This can't be happening.*

I was confused, I hadn't been asleep but my mind was confused.

I hadn't fully undressed for bed. I hadn't expected to sleep that night. I'd been writing in my journal of the afternoon I'd followed Dorcas into the village—or trying to write. The pen kept slipping from my hand. My eyes kept shutting. I was groggy now, and as terrified as any other resident of Heath Cottage. It was a shock to me to step outside and feel the nakedness of my close-cropped head, the exposed nape of my neck.

My hair? What had happened to my hair?

153

We were herded away from the house. We reassembled in the road. We stared back at our residence and saw no fire. Now it was revealed: the fire was elsewhere, a half-mile away. The fire was off-campus this time. One of the faculty houses on Brierly Lane. Above the burning house in the cul-de-sac of Brierly Lane the night sky glowed and pulsed. We stared in awe. We heard another emergency vehicle approach, siren blaring. We huddled together in jackets and coats hurriedly thrown over our nightclothes, bare feet kicked desperately into boots. Most of us were bareheaded. The wind whipped at our faces. We smelled smoke, we tasted soot. Adrenaline flooded our young bodies like liquid flame.

Panic made us festive, silly. Dominique cried, 'Jill-y, girl, look at *you*.' She swooped upon me, grabbed me and licked away my frost-tears with her soft warm tongue.

I laughed, taken so by surprise.

I couldn't bear to see Dominique's face.

I saw in her eyes the fear, and the elation.

It's their house isn't it? Burning.

There was Penelope, there was Cassie, there was Dominique, there was Gillian. Gripping one another's hands. Proctors were shouting at us to please return to our residence, the fire was elsewhere. 'You're in no danger. Repeat: no danger. Heath isn't on fire. The fire is off-campus. The fire is contained. Repeat: please return to your rooms.'

Someone, it might've been Cassie, squeezed my hand so hard I winced. She helped me up the front steps. Trooping back upstairs she helped me. I wanted to lie down on the stairs and sleep, I was so exhausted suddenly. We were back inside the residence by 4:10 A.M.

It wasn't true that the fire at 99 Brierly Lane had been 'contained.' It would burn out of control for more than an hour. Art supplies on the first floor would go up rapidly in flame; virtually none of Dorcas's totemic wooden figures would survive. The sculptress herself would die in the blaze, trapped in a second-floor bedroom with her husband, Andre Harrow, who would be removed from the fire still living, but who would die shortly afterward without regaining consciousness, in the intensive care unit in the Great Barrington hospital.

Because of isolated acts of arson on the Catamount campus, arson was suspected. But fire inspectors would conclude that the fire had probably been caused by a smoldering cigarette in a sofa downstairs.

These facts, I wouldn't learn for some time. That night after Cassie helped me back to my room I crawled into bed and slept for twelve hours.

24. *Paris, France*

Walking blindly along the Seine embankment, hardly aware of my surroundings, I was thinking of these events.

Unconsciously I touched my head beneath the woolen cloche hat I was wearing. Since the age of twenty I'd kept my hair trimmed short, the nape of my neck free. I hated hair in my eyes, and I hated the feel of it, sticky in warm weather, like someone's fingers, on my neck.

I smiled. I'd forgotten how the braids were burned, in that fire. How they must have blazed, like something festive. Before the totem itself caught fire.

I graduated from Catamount College, with honors, in 1977.

The Catamount College arsonist of 1974-1975 was never identified. Generally, it was believed that Marisa Spires was guilty. But a few months after the fire on Brierly Lane, two fifteen-year-old local boys were caught setting a fire behind the Catamount High School, three miles from campus; the fire resembled the Catamount campus fires, set with oily rags. The boys confessed to the campus fires, then retracted their confessions; later, they pleaded guilty to several of the fires, and received brief

157

sentences in a local juvenile facility.

In November 1976, a fire set with oily rags blazed out of control in a rowhouse in downtown Catamount, killing a woman and two young children; police investigated a number of suspects including the woman's estranged husband, but there were no arrests, finally, for lack of evidence. And after that, so far as I knew, the Catamount arsons ceased permanently.

The day swiftly waned. The sun had never appeared except as a vague haze; now it disappeared completely into night. But the lights of the embankment came on. Streetlamps, headlights. A stream of lights. I stood on the embankment staring at the Eiffel Tower on the far side of the river; the tower was bedecked in lights that, every hour, were timed to 'incandesce.' Tourists stared, and took photos. It was a fairy-tale spectacle to make you smile.

'*Belle*, yes?'

A woman spoke to me, standing close beside me. I looked, and it was Dominique.

We were in Paris for eight days, staying at the small French hotel on the rue Cassette where we usually stayed in Paris. Dominique was a choreographer for the Alvin Ailey Dance Theater where she'd been a dancer through her twenties; I was provost of a small, but distinguished, liberal arts college in suburban Philadelphia. We often traveled together, though we lived apart.

Dominique squeezed my hand, to tease an answer from me. I laughed.

'Yes, *très belle.*'